THE ASSASSIN STRIKES!

Big Tree shrugged off his serape in an eyeblink, freeing his arms and exposing the long, single-edged knife in his sash. No one even appeared to notice as he cocked his right arm back and hurled the deadly weapon with lethal accuracy straight toward Touch the Sky.

But one person had noticed. Just as the knife was released, Little Bear's warning roar rose above the din of camp. Hearing it, Honey Eater acted instinctively.

Almost as if it were one long movement, Big Tree tossed the lead line free and leaped onto his pony. Touch the Sky was just in time to recognize his enemy, even as, from the corner of his eye, he saw something hurtling toward him.

An eyeblink later, just as the well-thrown knife should have punctured Touch the Sky's vitals, Honey Eater flew between him and the blade. A feral cry of misery and fear rose from Touch the Sky when he heard the sickening sound of the blade slicing into Honey Eater. Even as the lightning-fast pony raced from camp, bearing Big Tree to freedom, Touch the Sky's wife collapsed in his arms.

The *Cheyenne* Series:

CHEYENNE

DESERT MANHUNT

JUDD COLE

LEISURE BOOKS   **L**   NEW YORK CITY

A LEISURE BOOK®

June 1997

Published by

Dorchester Publishing Co., Inc.
276 Fifth Avenue
New York, NY 10001

DESERT MANHUNT

Prologue

Although Matthew Hanchon bore the name given to him by his adopted white parents, he was the son of full-blooded Northern Cheyennes. The lone survivor of a bluecoat massacre in 1840, the infant was raised by John and Sarah Hanchon in the Wyoming Territory settlement of Bighorn Falls.

His parents loved him as their own, and at first the youth was happy enough in his limited world. The occasional stares and threats from others meant little—until his sixteenth year and a forbidden love with Kristen, daughter of the wealthy rancher Hiram Steele.

Steele's campaign to run Matthew off like a distempered wolf was assisted by Seth Carlson, the jealous, Indian-hating cavalry officer who was in love with Kristen. Carlson delivered a fateful ultimatum: Either Matthew cleared out of Bighorn

7

Falls for good, or Carlson would ruin his parents' contract to supply nearby Fort Bates—and thus ruin their mercantile business.

His heart sad but determined, Matthew set out for the upcountry of the Powder River, Cheyenne territory. Captured by braves from Chief Yellow Bear's tribe, he was declared an Indian spy for the hair-face soldiers and was brutally tortured over fire. But only a heartbeat before he was to be scalped and gutted, old Arrow Keeper interceded.

The tribe shaman and protector of the sacred Medicine Arrows, Arrow Keeper had recently experienced an epic vision. This vision foretold that the long-lost son of a great Cheyenne chief would return to his people—and that he would lead them in one last, great victory against their enemies. This youth would be known by the distinctive mark of the warrior, the same birthmark Arrow Keeper spotted buried past this youth's hairline: a mulberry-colored arrowhead.

Arrow Keeper used his influence to spare the youth's life. He also ordered that he be allowed to join the tribe, training with the junior warriors. This infuriated two braves especially: the fierce war leader, Black Elk, and his cunning younger cousin, Wolf Who Hunts Smiling.

Black Elk was jealous of the glances cast at the tall young stranger by Honey Eater, daughter of Chief Yellow Bear. And Wolf Who Hunts Smiling, proudly ambitious despite his youth, hated all whites without exception. This stranger was, to him, only a make-believe Cheyenne who wore white man's shoes, spoke the paleface tongue, and showed his emotions in his face like the woman-hearted white men.

Arrow Keeper buried the stranger's white name forever and gave him a new Cheyenne name: Touch the Sky. But he remained a white man's dog in the eyes of many in the tribe. At first humiliated at every turn, eventually the determined youth mastered the warrior arts. Slowly, as his coup stick filled with enemy scalps, he won the respect of more and more in the tribe.

But with each victory, deceiving appearances triumphed over reality, and the acceptance he so desperately craved eluded him. Worse, his hard-won victories left him with two especially fierce enemies outside the tribe: a Blackfoot called Sis-ki-dee and a Comanche named Big Tree.

As for Black Elk, at first he was hard but fair. When Touch the Sky rode off to save his white parents from outlaws, Honey Eater was convinced that he had deserted her and the tribe forever. She was forced to accept Black Elk's bride-price after her father crossed to the Land of Ghosts. But Touch the Sky returned.

Then, as it became clear to all that Honey Eater loved only Touch the Sky, Black Elk's jealousy drove him to join his younger cousin in plotting against Touch the Sky's life. Finally, Wolf Who Hunts Smiling's treachery forced a crisis: Aiming at Touch the Sky in heavy fog, he instead killed Black Elk. Now Touch the Sky stood accused of the murder in the eyes of many.

Though it divided the tribe irrevocably, he and Honey Eater performed the squaw-taking ceremony. He had firm allies in his blood brother Little Horse, the youth Two Twists, and Tangle Hair. Following Arrow Keeper's mysterious disappearance, Touch the Sky became the tribe shaman.

But a pretend shaman named Medicine Flute, backed by Touch the Sky's enemies, challenged his authority. And despite his fervent need to stop being the eternal outsider, Touch the Sky was still trapped between two worlds, welcome in neither.

Chapter One

"Brother," Little Horse said, "there may be hope for this tribe yet."

These unexpected words made the tall, broad-shouldered warrior called Touch the Sky pull up short. The two Cheyenne braves were walking across the central camp clearing toward the common corral.

"Buck," Touch the Sky said, "some in this tribe call me White Man Runs Him, but others call me Shaman. Yet you are the one speaking riddles. Old Arrow Keeper taught me there is *always* hope in the breast of a warrior. I never questioned that you are indeed a warrior, and none better between where we stand now and the Marias River. So give tongue to this hope of yours. I would gladly hear of it."

Little Horse nodded. All around them, the lush

new grass of the snow-melt moons was springing up. The winter-starved ponies, gaunt and weak from gnawing on cottonwood bark all winter, were putting meat on their bones. Bright-colored wildflowers dotted the meadows, and the ice-locked valleys were once again rich with wild game.

"I do not suggest," Little Horse said, "that we are not still a tribe dangerously divided against itself. We are. The Bullwhip soldiers swear allegiance to Wolf Who Hunts Smiling and his pretend shaman, the cowardly Medicine Flute. The Bowstring soldiers are loyal to Chief River of Winds and you. We are still a powder keg, and it could go off anytime."

Touch the Sky's lips tilted into a grim smile. He wore his hair in long, loose locks except where it was cut short over his eyes to clear his vision. Little Horse, in contrast, wore his hair in a single braid tied with red strings.

"As you say, we are a powder keg," Touch the Sky agreed. "So why sing of hope?"

They had resumed walking. All around them the women and children scurried, for the finishing touches were being added to the Northern Cheyenne summer camp at the confluence of the Powder and Little Powder rivers. Tipis had been erected in clan circles, with their entrances all facing east toward the birthplace of Sister Sun. But the meat racks still had to be built in preparation for the spring hunt.

"Only notice something, brother," Little Horse said. "True, you can look down toward the river and see all our enemies congregated around Medicine Flute's tipi. But have you looked closely at them?"

Touch the Sky did just that. Then he said, "Crack the nut and expose the meat. I still see no clear signs of hope."

Indeed, even as he spoke, one of those around Medicine Flute's tipi caught his eye: a small but muscle-hardened warrior with swift, furtive eyes—eyes that remained constantly in motion, on guard for the ever-expected attack. But they slowed down now long enough to beam pure hatred at Touch the Sky.

Wolf Who Hunts Smiling. But his name fell short of his treachery, for Touch the Sky knew from bitter experience there was no evil deed beyond this Wolf's doing.

"You do not see it?" said an incredulous Little Horse. "You, who can find sign on a hardpan canyon floor? Brother, there is something very different. Look at them. They are gambling, whittling arrow points, drinking corn beer. See Hawk Trainer over there? He is playing with his bird. What are they usually up to when they congregate after the cold moons?"

Slowly his friend's point sank home. Touch the Sky nodded, for he knew quite well what his enemies were usually up to.

"By custom," he answered, "they should be huddled in council. Scheming. Plotting the overthrow of this camp."

Little Horse nodded. "As you say. Notice how few of them are bothering to watch our movements. Usually they stay on you, me, Tangle Hair, and Two Twists like vultures on carrion. And earlier today, when Two Twists rode out on herd guard—none of the Whips harassed him as they usually do."

Touch the Sky considered all this. By now the two braves had reached the buffalo-hair rope corral. It held only the favorite mounts of the braves, for each man had as many as ten ponies on his string, and the rest were allowed to range free under a herd guard.

"And consider Wendigo Mountain," Little Horse continued. "You heard the word-bringer from Red Shale. Since your bluecoat friend Tom Riley led his pony soldiers against the renegades camped on Wendigo Mountain, Big Tree's Comanches and Sis-ki-dee's Blackfoot marauders have been routed from their bastion. No one has seen them for several moons."

"Yes," Touch the Sky said quietly. "No one has seen them."

Something in his tone gave Little Horse pause. But the short, stoutly muscled warrior went on. "And with the renegades routed, Wolf Who Hunts Smiling is afraid to strike. He needs his allies to ensure the fight here in camp. All these reasons, shaman, seem to me fodder for hope."

Touch the Sky always listened closely when Little Horse spoke, for his friend was a man of few words. It was Little Horse's way to pay attention only to things that mattered.

"You could be right, stout fighter," the tall brave conceded. He gave a sharp whistle, and a powerfully muscled coyote dun broke from the rest of the ponies, trotting over to greet him by nuzzling his shoulder.

Little Horse recognized the doubt in his friend's voice. "I could be, you are saying, but you do not think so?"

"No, brother, I do not. First of all, as to *those* jays"—Touch the Sky nodded across toward the Bullwhips—"they are distracted now, in an especially good mood, because our trade goods are due to arrive soon."

Little Horse nodded, for he had forgotten this point. Every year the Far West Mining Company sent a huge shipment of trade goods by pack train to the Northern Cheyenne camp. This was the annual payment, arranged by Touch the Sky, for Cheyenne permission to haul the miners' gold ore across Cheyenne ranges. The arrival of the goods was always a festive occasion rivaling the Spring Dance.

"As for our enemies on Wendigo Mountain," Touch the Sky went on, "I was almost happier when we knew where they were. When it comes to that bunch, you are in trouble when you see them and in greater trouble when you don't."

All of this sobered Little Horse. His friend was right, and he knew it. Touch the Sky quickly inspected his dun's hooves while Little Horse leaped onto his bay and ran him around the corral a few laps to work out the kinks.

Touch the Sky tweaked the dun's ears fondly while glancing back toward camp. A small group of children were playing war near the river. Touch the Sky watched the boys counting coup on each other with willow branches and realized, his pride mixed with sadness, that they were not playing at all. This was the vital early training in warfare that would continue until they were well beyond their fortieth winter—assuming they survived that long.

One of the boys, younger than the rest but sturdy and fast, suddenly roared with ferocious triumph as he counted coup. Touch the Sky felt an ear-to-ear smile stretch his face, and pride swelled his throat. It was that roar that had earned his son his first name in life: Little Bear—the name given to him by his parents, the name that would be replaced once more in life when he earned his warrior's name.

Absorbed in watching his son, Touch the Sky did not realize that his friend had returned quietly to his side.

"You are watching your boy," Little Horse said. "And thinking of that boy's mother. That is why you find it so much harder to find hope. I have no child to bounce on my knee, or woman to feed. My world is an easier place than yours."

Touch the Sky shook his head. "Your world *could* be easier. You could live free and easy, and top any woman who was for the taking. Instead, you fight my battles with me, and Maiyun knows I have battles enough for ten men. Yes, my world is a hard place. But I am not moaning." He met his friend's eye. "Not moaning," he repeated. "Just worried. Arrow Keeper appeared to me in a dream last night."

Little Horse's copper skin paled a shade. No one could say for sure if Arrow Keeper, tribe shaman before Touch the Sky, was in the Land of Ghosts.

He had simply disappeared one day. But it was sure—sure as death itself—that he never appeared to Touch the Sky unless serious trouble was in the wind.

Little Horse had to lick his lips before he could speak. His words were almost a whisper. "What did he say?"

Only now, when Touch the Sky finally answered, did Little Horse fully comprehend his friend's despondency.

"He told me," Touch the Sky replied tonelessly, "that the worst hurt in the world is coming for me."

The Wyoming Territory river-bend settlement called Bighorn Falls was located one day's hard ride south of the Cheyenne summer camp. Treaties signed earlier at Fort Laramie had established an uneasy peace between white settlers and the local tribes, among whom the Sioux and their Cheyenne cousins dominated in this area.

But "peace" was a word written on water. Both sides had shown bad faith. White miners, forbidden by treaty from prospecting the sacred Black Hills, had gone in anyway. Renegade Indians, in turn, had attacked whites and stolen their property.

All this tumbled through his thoughts as the grizzled former mountain man called Old Knobby watched the pack train below him.

The old trapper had known, as soon as he spotted the long line of sweating bull-whackers, who they were. Bearing north, horses and mules and even a few oxen yoked Mexican fashion were all loaded high with trade goods.

"Heap big doin's up Powder River way," he informed his horse, a big claybank mare grazing behind him on a grassy ridge overlooking Bighorn Falls. "Them goods is for Matthew's tribe."

New calico cloth, he thought. Powder, lead, and balls for the upcoming hunts. Steel knives, sulfur matches, mirrors, combs, flour, sugar, coffee—after a winter of pemmican and yarrow tea, those goods would be like rain to dry earth. All because Matthew had put his bacon in the fire once again for his people. Yet the red men didn't want him any more than the white men did.

"It's a goddamn pisspot of a world," Knobby informed his mare. The old man was somewhat ashamed of riding a mare in this wild country where only women and children would be seen on one. But the claybank had endless stamina and a gentle gait that was easy on Old Knobby's rheumatism. Like all former mountain men, he talked to his animals as if they were people.

Knobby watched the long pack train snake its way across the wide gravel ford just north of town. Curious onlookers had gathered to watch them, though the bull-whackers were such a rough crowd of half-breeds and hard cases that women were hustling the younger boys away.

Old Knobby chuckled at the sight. He could hear the teamsters cussing even from here. They reminded him of the old Green River Rendezvous days. One of the heavily burdened mules had managed to lie down. That meant it had to be un-packed again so that it could stand.

Knobby shook his head again as the cussed irony of it hit him. Matthew or Touch the Sky or whatever the hell you called him, that red son had grown up here in the Falls. The Hanchons raised him like their own blood, and he loved them back the same. Only one full day's ride between them, but it might as well be the entire Pacific Ocean.

The Hanchons had been good to Knobby after he proved his loyalty to their adopted boy. When his fondness for wagon-yard whiskey cost him his job as hostler in town, John and Sarah Hanchon took him on at their mustang spread. He was too damned old and stove up for the hard work. But Knobby had proven invaluable to the younger hands, showing them how to break green horses to leather. He was also a good line guard when the horses were up in their summer pastures as they were now.

The old man was about to turn away and ride back to his shack to boil some coffee. But just then something caught his eye below.

Knobby squinted, studying the scene even more closely. The old man removed his flap hat, revealing the silver-dollar-size raw spot on his crown—a Cheyenne warrior had started to scalp him until the trapper let daylight into his soul with a pepperbox pistol.

"Well, cuss my coup," he said finally, convinced. His hearing was starting to go, he was sprung in the knees, and he was growing long in the tooth. But Old Knobby could still see like a young eagle.

And he had definitely gotten a good look when that last bull-whacker paused at the river, removed his wide felt hat, and mopped the sweat from his face.

His Injun face, Knobby thought.

That in itself was not unusual. Many of the teamsters were 'breeds, and plenty of Indians hired on with white freighting companies. But Knobby was sure he had recognized this Indian—recognized his broad, homely Comanche features and short hair parted exactly in the middle.

"Hellfire and corruption," he swore softly to his mare. "We got a herring in the pickle barrel, Fireaway. That ain't no freighter. That's that sneaky Comanche bastard Big Tree, and I'll be et fir a tater if he ain't planning to send Matthew across the great divide!"

Knobby didn't stop to wonder how in hell the renegade got mixed in with the freighters. Hell, maybe Hiram Steele arranged it. That hidebound son of a bitch had had blood in his eye for Matthew ever since the youth had the audacity to fall in love with Steele's daughter, Kristen.

The why of it didn't matter now. Knobby knew he had to get word to Matthew somehow. The best man to send would be Corey Robinson, Matt's old boyhood chum. But Corey was laid up with that leg he busted in a fall from his horse.

"Looks like it's me and you, girl," Knobby said to his mare. He didn't look forward to such a long ride to the upcountry of the Powder. But he could be spared, and besides, an old coot on a mare was beneath the dignity of most warriors—he stood a good chance of crossing Indian ranges unmolested, especially as he spoke Sioux and knew sign talk.

"Let's go shake the oat bag," he told his claybank. "One good feed, girl, then we got us a hard ride. There's trouble on the spit."

Chapter Two

"The pack train is closer!" shouted an old grandmother of the Antelope Eaters Clan. She had run down to the river to spread the word. "The Lakota at Medicine Bend Creek have sent mirror flashes. It passed there."

"The moccasin telegraph is quick," Two Twists said bitterly to Touch the Sky, looking toward the Bullwhip lodge. "When you made medicine with the white miners, the Whips and their lickspittles called you White Man Runs Him and a traitor. They still use that as fodder when they are singing the litany of your supposed sins. But look now! They plan to be first in line when the goods are distributed. These mighty warriors have mighty mouths! They talk one way, but behave many."

Touch the Sky nodded, for all of it was spoken

straight arrow. He, Honey Eater, and Little Bear, surrounded by Touch the Sky's loyal band of three, sat near the water. Honey Eater's aunt, Sharp Nosed Woman, had joined them. Little Bear, just shy of his fourth winter now, frolicked in the water, using a log for a canoe. The two women were shelling wild peas into a battered metal pot. The men filed arrow points and crimped shells or worked on cleaning and repairing their weapons.

"They are bald hypocrites," Touch the Sky agreed. "But each item they add to their hoard makes it harder for them to paint the white settlers black. Let them speak two ways, so long as they confine their 'boldness' to their words."

Tangle Hair, who rivaled Little Horse in taciturnity, nodded at this. "I am indifferent to most of the goods," he boasted, though he added as an afterthought, "Except for the sugar and coffee. But only look up at the camp. Touch the Sky has created another annual festival for the Shaiyena tribe."

It was true. A festival spirit dominated camp. The women had put on their best cloth dresses, adorned with all manner of jewelry and feathers and bright coins, including Presidential Medals with engravings of the Great White Father.

"Yes," Touch the Sky said, watching his wife and child. "It has brought a little peace, if only for a time."

Honey Eater knew the custom, of course, and would never have spoken to join a conversation of men. But her eyes met her husband's, and he saw that she, too, shared in his belief.

Again Touch the Sky felt it, even after years of living with this woman: that stirring of belly flies inside at the power of her beauty. The skin flawless and smooth as wild honey; the big, obsidian eyes shaped like wing tips; the beautiful, glossy mass of her hair, white columbine petals threaded through it. In a tribe famous for its beauties, still this one stood out.

But again his mind returned to the memory of Arrow Keeper, like a tongue returning to a broken tooth. *The worst hurt in the world is coming.* The wording was important. Arrow Keeper did not say "trouble." He said "hurt." Touch the Sky had learned a long time ago that, for him and those fool enough to follow him, the end of one battle only marked the beginning of the next. Suffering and pain had become close companions.

But the strongest man in the world was soft somewhere, he thought, glancing at his wife and child. He found some comfort when he reminded himself that they should be safe. No man had truer friends, or better fighters for companions, than he did. Every man in his band would unhesitatingly die to save Honey Eater or Little Bear.

"Brother," Little Horse said, as if divining his friend's thoughts from his troubled eyes, "I recalled a thing this morning. I recalled how Seth Carlson and Hiram Steele once used the pack train to slip an infected blanket into this camp. You will be serving as interpreter. May I suggest a thing? Before we touch any of the goods, make sure the freighters will also touch them."

Touch the Sky nodded, grinning. "I will,

brother. And the first who refuses will watch the camp dogs eat his entrails."

Touch the Sky had run through the list of his enemies—the leaders of the pack, at any rate. Seth Carlson, the bluecoat pony soldier who was convinced Touch the Sky had stolen Kristen Steele from him; Hiram Steele himself, obsessed with the false idea that his daughter had been topped by a red man; Big Tree, the Comanche terror from the Blanco Canyon; Sis-ki-dee, the Blackfoot madman known widely as the Red Peril; and closest to home, the cunning and ambitious Wolf Who Hunts Smiling.

He had faced each of them separately, and all of them at once, and still they had not killed him. But neither had he lessened their numbers. He had killed their white gunslicks and red toadies, but the five remained—all of them, poised to strike at any time.

"Hii-ya! Hii-*ya*!"

The Cheyenne war cry. Hearing it startled Touch the Sky out of his reverie. Everyone on the bank stared out toward the river.

Little Bear had come up with a "spear" somewhere, a stick with a blunt point at one end. As the rest watched, he again shouted the war cry as he leaped from his canoe, attempting to spear a trout.

The clumsy little mite missed by a stone's throw. But his serious war face and the energy of his attempt impressed the men on the bank, who all loosed a mighty cheer of admiration. Even the women suspended modesty and joined the cheer.

Again Touch the Sky's eyes met those of his wife. She smiled at him, a smile that encouraged him to take hope.

Hope. He tried to school himself in that thought. But the sere, cracked, wind-rawed face of Arrow Keeper stayed with him. So did the whispered word, sinister and foreboding: *hurt*.

Old Knobby's spirits were in far better shape than his sitter.

He had taken a great chance and ridden north all through the night, knowing the slower pack train would make camp at sunset. Since he had a comfortable jump on them, the old trapper held his claybank to nothing faster than an easy trot. Assisted by a generous moon and an explosion of stars, he followed the Old Lakota Trace, which he had not ridden in twenty years.

God-in-whirlwinds! he thought. The West, while still far from tame, was already starting to simmer down from the wild-and-woolly days he remembered. Hell, there was a way station up on Beaver Creek now—part of the new short-line stage service from Laramie and Register Cliffs. And homesteaders on the old buffalo ranges! Why, the damned hoe-men were even putting up fences to protect their crops.

"Damn tarnal foolishness, Fireaway," Knobby assured the claybank mare as they came up out of a cutbank. "It's got so's a man can't eat good meat 'less he pays a goddamn tax on it."

Old Knobby never thought it would come to this: to actually feeling *sorry* the old dangers were gone. But the old dangers had always been exaggerated—it was the old freedoms he missed. From the Cumberland Gap to South Pass, only the names changed—the desire for freedom was constant. Men pushed on west to get away from cussed "syphilization." From its foolish laws and cowardly restrictions and womanish fussing.

The claybank abruptly stopped and crow-hopped slightly off the trail. Knobby was instantly alert, searching the moonlit darkness around him.

But it was only some settler's hound dog, and a friendly one at that. Knobby could count its ribs—evidently it had strayed too far from home.

Feeling sorry for it, he drew a cold corn dodger from the fiber sack tied to his saddle horn.

"Wrap your teeth around that, old campaigner," he said, tossing the food to the hound.

Why, hell, Knobby thought again as he pressured the mare with his knees, resuming the journey north to the Powder River country of the Cheyennes. A damned dog! Used to was, a man might meet up with a silvertip bear hereabouts.

Still . . . this easy journey meant a timely warning for Matthew and his tribe. Knobby knew that was most important. And right now, he was way ahead of that two-faced, back-stabbing, conniving Comanche devil Big Tree. Knobby would be in plenty of time to warn Matthew.

Was it the whole damned shebang? Knobby wondered. Were they *all* in on it—the entire pack train? Were they all going to strike once inside the camp? That didn't seem likely. Among tribes renowned for making fierce stands in their very camps, Cheyennes were second to none. Even the women and children would pitch into the fight. Besides, they'd be ready.

No. The old man shook his head, digging at a tick in his beard. No—Big Tree was sneaking in to kill one Indian, and that Indian was Matt Hanchon, better known these days as Touch the Sky of the Northern Cheyenne.

While he rode, the old trailsman let his mind roam free, recalling his days and nights in the awesome Great Stony Mountains, now called the Rockies by greenhorns. Funny how making this ride brought back all the old ways and lore. He even remembered his first lesson in survival, taught by the legendary Caleb Greenwood himself: "When it's cold, walk in the shade. When it's hot, walk in the sun. That way you'll never meet a snake."

The claybank shied and again crow-hopped sideways.

"Gee up there, girl," Knobby scoffed at his mount. "It's just 'at ol' hound, following our back trail."

Knobby figured to get word to Matthew, rest up a few hours while his horse grazed, and then return before John Hanchon missed him. John and Sarah already had grief enough, worrying about their adopted boy. Lord knows they saw him seldom enough. Sarah, especially, would take it hard if Knobby had to explain that Big Tree was out for Matt's hair—Big Tree, the same red devil who had planted an arrow in Sarah's back.

"H'ar now!" the old man grumbled when the claybank again started fighting him. "We got to git, Fireaway!"

It was that damned hound. Knobby had two guns in his twin saddle boots—the old Kentucky over-and-under he called Patsy Plumb and a weak scattergun loaded with buckshot, used mainly for close-in defense when he was surprised.

It wasn't his way to waste a shot. But this trip was turning into a Sunday stroll, so he could afford it. He had to scare off that hound, or the mare would be fidgety the whole damn way. Besides, the buckshot wouldn't seriously hurt at this range—only sting and scare.

Knobby halted his mare, slid the gun from its boot, grunting with the effort as he slewed around in the saddle. Aiming to one side of the hound's shadowy form, he squeezed off the load.

The exploding gun sent the dog scrambling and made the claybank jump a bit. "There, you damned nancy," Old Knobby said, turning back around. "Now, git—"

A sudden orange flash exploded inside Knobby's skull, pain made him cry out, and the force of the surprise blow knocked the old man out of his saddle. He had enough presence of mind and strength left to grab his rigging as he slid down, breaking his fall.

Knobby balanced on the feather edge of awareness, pain thudding in his skull like tom-toms. He lay half on the ground, his legs caught in the twisted stirrups and latigos. His flap hat slid away from his eyes, and he saw them peering down at him, one holding the mare's bridle: Indians!

They laughed in scorn, one pointing at his horse. What kind of man would ride a mare?

He recognized them as Digger Indians from

their filthy hides and tangled, dirty hair. The notorious thieves from the Missouri River country, pushed west by land-hungry whites. Maybe he could palaver with them, make medicine. Maybe—

One of the Diggers again slammed the stout tree branch into the old man's head, and Knobby's world closed down to pain and darkness.

When the camp crier announced that the pack train had crossed Weeping Woman Ridge, Touch the Sky and his comrades went into action.

The Bullwhips and the Bowstrings, the tribe's two soldier societies, were its official policemen. It was their job to be on guard when any outsiders entered camp. And Touch the Sky knew outsiders were expected, especially the Bowstrings, who were mostly loyal to Chief River of Winds and the Law-ways, as well as the Council of Forty.

But the Bullwhips, most of them lickspittles of Wolf Who Hunts Smiling, could not be trusted. Yes, they would have their weapons to hand—but who knew which side they would join if fighting broke out? To counter that possibility, Touch the Sky and his band—the equal of any forty men— would be ready to assist the Bowstrings.

Honey Eater did not need to be told how critical this time was. She would hang back, keeping Little Bear with her, until Touch the Sky had made his initial inspection of the arriving party. Only then would she and the rest of the women and children and elders be called out by the camp crier.

The soldiers cleared the camp clearing of excited Indians, the Bullwhips occasionally resorting to their dreaded whips when someone lagged behind.

Eventually the clearing was empty except for the armed braves. They watched the long pack train snake its way down the ridge outside camp, flying a white truce flag. Cheyennes kept many camp dogs for security, and they went wild now. Those with wolf in their blood snapped and howled fiercely until their owners hurled rocks in among them to quiet them down.

The leader of the pack train was wise in the ways of the red man. He stopped his caravan well outside of camp and sent a word-bringer ahead to request permission to enter. It was granted.

Touch the Sky made eye contact with his men: Little Horse, Two Twists, Tangle Hair, all strategically placed. As the first heavily laden pack animals trudged to a halt, his men all sent the same signal: No imminent signs of trouble. Touch the Sky saw how things were too. No freighter carried a weapon to hand, nor were any of them well-supplied with spare cartridges.

The leader, who had made this run three years in a row, raised one hand high in peace as he approached Touch the Sky. "Caleb Riley sends his regards," the teamster called out in English. "Said to tell you he added some of Gail Borden's new canned milk to the load. Says you're to try it in your coffee."

Touch the Sky could not help but grin as he greeted the man. The rest of the bull-whackers had entered the clearing and were hobbling their animals. Touch the Sky nodded to the camp crier.

He tore off down the paths, calling the rest out to admire the goods.

Even the most disciplined warriors began exclaiming and getting caught up in the excitement as the goods were heaped for inspection. Touch the Sky smiled, watching Honey Eater's eyes widen as she inspected a bolt of blue cotton cloth. One of the freighters, a friendly half-breed who liked children, was passing out licorice drops.

The clearing was humming with activity, streaming with Indians and freighters and animals. Touch the Sky was aware, without giving it much thought, that one of the freighters wore a serape and a big flap hat that left his face in shadows. The man caught his eye because of the powerful-looking pony tied by a lead line to his loaded mule. Perhaps he traded something for it at the Sioux Camp at Medicine Bend.

Touch the Sky turned away to translate something between the head freighter and Chief River of Winds. Big Tree chose that moment to strike.

The Comanche shrugged off the serape in an eyeblink, freeing his arms and exposing the long, single-edged knife in his sash. No one even appeared to notice as he cocked his right arm back and hurled the deadly weapon with lethal accuracy straight toward Touch the Sky.

But one person had noticed. Just as the knife was released, Little Bear's warning roar rose above the din of camp. Hearing it, Honey Eater reacted instinctively.

Almost as if it were all just one long movement, Big Tree tossed the lead line free and leaped onto the spare pony—one he had selected for speed and stamina. Touch the Sky was just in time to recognize his enemy, even as, from the corner of his eye, he saw something hurtling toward him.

An eyeblink later, just as the well-thrown knife should have punctured Touch the Sky's vitals, Honey Eater flew between him and the blade. A feral cry of misery and fear rose from Touch the Sky when he heard the sickening sound of the blade slicing into Honey Eater. Even as the lightning-fast pony raced from camp, bearing Big Tree to freedom, Touch the Sky's wife collapsed in his arms.

Chapter Three

Near chaos still gripped the Powder River camp when Wolf Who Hunts Smiling slipped out unseen.

His usually cunning features were now a mask of grim foreboding. As the people pressed closer to the center of the trouble, he exchanged quick nods with several of his toadies. Then, with Bull-whips forming a screen, he hurried down to the huge stands of cattails and reeds near the water.

It was the custom to make secret escape trails in case of surprise attack. Wolf Who Hunts Smiling hurried along one now, casting nervous backward glances.

His woman! That fool Big Tree had knifed Touch the Sky's woman—the very light of his life, she and that puling brat of theirs.

There was no man in the world Wolf Who Hunts

Smiling would not face, including the tall one. Indeed, he *had* faced Touch the Sky, more than once. Each had failed to kill the other—savage equals in a savage land.

But even Wolf Who Hunts Smiling would not lightly draw blood from the tall one's woman or child. Now it was imperative, the fleeing brave realized, that all of Touch the Sky's enemies band together and think like one man. Otherwise, they would all feel the deadly sting of his bottomless rage and *die* like one man.

He knew where Big Tree had ridden to—the prearranged spot where Big Tree, Wolf Who Hunts Smiling, and Sis-ki-dee were to meet after the killing of Touch the Sky. But that plan was smoke behind them now.

Wolf Who Hunts Smiling knew that Touch the Sky would not ride out immediately—his woman would come first.

But one of his deadly band might ride out. So now the Wolf hurried, fording the river once he was out of sight of camp and bearing toward the common corral from the west.

He gave a little whistle, and a pinto with a roached mane trotted over to him. Wolf Who Hunts Smiling grabbed a handful of mane stubble, swung onto his mount, and hunkered low over its neck. He urged the stallion northwest toward the tall, windswept pinnacle whites called Lookout Rock.

Sis-ki-dee, tears of amusement still streaming down his scar-pocked face, looked at Big Tree with mocking contempt.

"What, Quohada? Another dead woman on your string, and no hair to prove it? Perhaps you should ride back and ask Touch the Sky if you may scalp her before the funeral?"

Wolf Who Hunts Smiling, despite his apprehension, almost laughed outright at this. But Big Tree's scowl of rage checked him.

"Laugh, Red Peril. But up in Bloody Bones Canyon, you begged like a white man. Begged the tall shaman to spare your life. And he did, out of pure contempt, for his honor would not let him kill a coward."

The mirth fled from Sis-ki-dee's insane eyes, and for a moment Wolf Who Hunts Smiling was sure these two would kill each other. All three of them had sheltered in the lee of Lookout Rock. From here, a man could see anything approaching from any direction while it was still a long ride off.

"You two jays," the Wolf scoffed. "Are you women, trading insults in your sewing lodge? Have you eyes to see what has happened? Even now the woman of White Man Runs Him is dead or dying. I tell you now, and this place hears me, he saw Big Tree's face. And he will move heaven and earth to kill not only him, but anyone else involved in this."

These words sobered the other two like sharp slaps to the face.

"I will have to ride," Big Tree said. "And none can call me coward. Any man fool enough to face him now will die a dog's death."

Sis-ki-dee nodded. "The custom is clear. As the Wolf says, he will come for all of us. But he must start with the man who drew blood, and that is you, Quohada."

"It was Hiram Steele," Big Tree fumed. He shot an accusing stare at Wolf Who Hunts Smiling. "Every time you parley with hair-faces, we end up doing their donkey work. Now only look. Steele's trickery and bribes got me into that pack train—now he will stay back in the shadows while we fight the battle."

"So what?" Wolf Who Hunts Smiling shot back. "Why lick old wounds when it's time for action?"

"Is his she-bitch whore dead?" Sis-ki-dee demanded.

"She looked dead when I left," Wolf Who Hunts Smiling replied. "I could not see if it was a gut stab or higher in a lung. But the blood was copious."

"I will ride south to Blanco Canyon," Big Tree decided.

He meant the desolate spot, deep in the dead heart of the Llano Estacado or Staked Plains, that marked the homeland of the Quohada Comanches. It was many sleeps' hard ride from here, in the land of red rock canyons and burning alkali flats.

Wolf Who Hunts Smiling shook his head. "Good, but not good enough. He routed you out of the Blanco before. You must ride farther. Deep into the country of the Brown Ones. You speak their tongue, know their land. Touch the Sky does not."

By "the Brown Ones," Wolf Who Hunts Smiling meant the Mexicans. Big Tree did not argue, for his Cheyenne ally was right.

"I know a Mexican in Sonora," Big Tree said.

"His name is Poco Loco. He has a band of *pisto-leros* who have defeated even the famous Texas Rangers. I used to sell Indian slaves to him. He has a stronghold deep in the sierras. I will ride there."

Wolf Who Hunts Smiling approved this with a nod.

"What if his precious woman does not die?" Sis-ki-dee suggested.

"It matters not," the Wolf said. "I have already heard Touch the Sky make his vow publicly, with the Council of Forty as his witnesses. Any man who hurts his woman or whelp is marked for worm fodder. Ride, Big Tree, and lure him into Mexico. You are no second-line warrior, buck! He fears you, and rightly. Lure him into Mexico, and leave him there as carrion!"

Old Knobby looked about as miserable as Touch the Sky had ever seen him—perhaps almost as miserable as Touch the Sky himself felt, though that hardly seemed possible to the grief-stricken Cheyenne.

"Tarnal hell, Matthew," Knobby said awkwardly around the clay stem of Touch the Sky's best cal-umet, "I tried to get here in time. My hand to God! But them damned Diggers stripped me of every-thing I had. They boosted my hoss, too. But Fire-away was broke to hate the Injun smell, no offense. She bolted first chance, and somehow she found me. All they ended up gittin' was the clothes off my back."

Indeed, Knobby had ridden into a tense camp a short time ago wrapped in his own saddle blanket.

Now, thanks to Little Horse, who was about his size, Knobby had been outfitted with a leather shirt and a pair of blue kersey trousers taken from a dead soldier. Double-soled, knee-length elkskin moccasins covered his legs.

His mouth a grim, determined slit, Touch the Sky accepted the pipe from his old friend and set it on the ground between them. Both men sat over a glowing firepit in Touch the Sky's now-lonely tipi. By custom, the seriously wounded Honey Eater had been rushed to the women's sick lodge. No men would be allowed in while her clan grandmothers chanted the old cure songs. Little Bear was safe for the moment with the women of Honey Eater's clan.

"You don't have to make excuses to me, old-timer," Touch the Sky said. "Those bruises on your face are the color of grapes. I wish to God you could have gotten through, Knobby."

Again worry stabbed through him, and Touch the Sky fell silent, brooding. The only word he could obtain on Honey Eater came from her aunt Sharp Nosed Woman—and all she would do was shake her head sadly, muttering that it was up to the High Holy Ones now. The bleeding had been stemmed, and the wound packed with gentian and gunpowder.

"She gonna come sassy agin, tadpole?" Knobby asked quietly.

Touch the Sky's face was a study in abject misery. "There was so much blood lost," he said, his voice heavy with grief. "She took that knife for me, Knobby."

"H'ar now!" Knobby rebuked him, not liking the

dangerous, reckless gleam in the youth's eyes. "You got to hold the line now, boy. Your woman needs you, and you got you a pup on the robes now, too. Plenty of time later to settle the books with that red bastard Big Tree."

Touch the Sky nodded. "I don't set foot from this camp until . . . until I know about Honey Eater. One way or the other."

Knobby cut a strip from the hump steak he had cooked on the tripod outside the tipi entrance. His arrival had already occasioned slanted glances and hushed remarks from some of the others— remarks about Touch the Sky's loyalty to the hairfaces who were stealing their ranges. Others, however, had been impressed by the old trapper's obvious familiarity with Plains customs. His sign talk was proficient, and he knew quite a few Lakota words, a language understood by most Cheyennes.

Both men fell silent, watching orange spear-tips of flame dance in the pit. Touch the Sky sat with his Sharps carbine across his lap. One of his many enemies might well try to catch him off guard in his grief. Not that Touch the Sky feared death— but he was determined to live at least long enough to punish Big Tree and whoever else schemed with him in this.

"Brother!" came Little Horse's voice from outside. "I would speak with you."

Touch the Sky threw back the entrance flap and bade his friend enter.

"Well?" Touch the Sky demanded the moment Little Horse came in. This was proof the situation was serious, for no Cheyenne ever opened serious conversation without smoking to the directions and making inconsequential talk first.

"Big Tree rode toward Lookout Rock. I followed his trail long enough to verify it."

"And Wolf Who Hunts Smiling?"

"No one saw him ride out," Little Horse said. "Nor return. But his favorite pinto is lathered—I checked. He rode out, also."

"He was in on it," Touch the Sky said. "And Hiram Steele."

Knobby understood none of this except Hiram Steele's name. Touch the Sky translated.

"Wolf Who Hunts Smiling," Knobby repeated. "Ain't he the shifty-eyed one? That tough little buck what was on Wes Munro's keelboat with us?"

Touch the Sky nodded. "A low-crawling pig's afterbirth who sheds tribal blood."

"Ain't nobody lower than Big Tree," Knobby muttered. "Son of a bitch shot your ma in the back, and now he's hurt your wife. We've left that bastard off his leash too long already, Matthew."

While Knobby spoke, Little Horse watched his best friend rummage in a pile of buffalo robes near the center pole of the tipi. Little Horse frowned deeply when he saw what Touch the Sky drew out: a simple leather harness attached to several sharp steel hooks.

Old Knobby, who had spent years among the red men, recognized it too. His face paled behind his beard.

"Hell 'n' furies, sprout! You fixin' to set up a pole?"

Touch the Sky nodded. "I will hang from it through the night," he said in Cheyenne to Little

Horse. "Will you come cut me down at sunrise?"

With evident reluctance, Little Horse nodded. He had seen Touch the Sky go through this grueling voluntary ordeal before. "Setting up a pole" was a penance designed to propitiate the Holy Ones and sway them toward mercy on their red children. Touch the Sky would drive those steel hooks through his chest muscles—deep into the muscles. Then, his weight suspended in the harness, he would hang from a tall pole set up on a hill overlooking camp. The ordeal could kill even a strong man.

But neither Little Horse nor Knobby foolishly tried to talk Touch the Sky out of this move. His wife lay dying, her lifeblood drained from her. The look in Touch the Sky's eyes was a warning: He would brook interference from no man, not where his wife was concerned.

"Not only will I cut you down, shaman," Little Horse promised. "I will be out there with you on the hill through the night. There is nothing your enemies would like better than to gut you while you hang helpless."

Chapter Four

It was one of the longest, most agonizing nights of his hard life.

Touch the Sky had withstood the fiery pain in silence as he gouged the sharp hooks deep into his muscles. His face pouring sweat, he maintained that silence as Little Horse and Knobby rigged him to the pole and lowered it into its hole.

The pain of his weight pulling against those strained and tortured muscles verged on unbearable. All through the long night, Touch the Sky drifted in and out of consciousness like a man riding through a patchy fog.

By strict custom, his friends could gather near, but they could do nothing whatsoever to help alleviate his suffering. While he hung in that painful state, his mind drifting free, Touch the Sky saw many faces, heard many voices.

But one face kept returning to mock him, a grinning, ugly face streaked with the yellow and green war paint of the Comanches. Big Tree. The Red Raider of the Plains. Terrorizer of white settlers in Texas, now a nemesis of the red men on the Northern Plains. A brave man but without honor, a superb warrior but one without the compassion of all true warriors—and thus, one who counted women and children as "kills" along with the men he had slaughtered.

And while Touch the Sky hung there, balanced between life and death, Arrow Keeper's words returned from the hinterland of memory: *The worst hurt in the world is coming.*

Brother?

Touch the Sky?

Wake up, Matthew, wake

"—up, boy! Matthew! You hear me, tadpole?"

Slowly, like a sluggish snake after a cold night, Touch the Sky's mind returned to awareness.

He lay in the dew-tinted grass. Pain exploded in his chest with each heartbeat. Clean cloths had been tied over his bleeding wounds.

His friends circled him: Little Horse, Tangle Hair, Two Twists, Old Knobby. Worry was starched into their features. Two Twists made him drink a little hot tea from a clay bowl.

Golden splashes of morning sunlight dotted the grass. Touch the Sky tried to sit up, but it felt as if six-inch spikes were being kicked into his chest.

"Easy, buck," Little Horse cautioned him.

Touch the Sky tried to speak, but failed. He drank a little more of the tea. Then he licked his cracked lips and tried again. "Honey Eater?" he managed.

Little Horse shook his head. "We have waited with you, shaman. We will learn her fate at your side."

It took infinite effort for Touch the Sky to rise, even with the help of his friends.

"We will stop at Hawk Woman's tipi first," he said wearily. "I will get my son, too. Whatever the truth, he too will face it like a man."

Slowly, with many in camp looking on in sympathy, others with contempt, Touch the Sky's friends helped him down the hill and back into camp. Little Bear, who had been up almost all night worrying about his hurt mother, was sound asleep.

Tangle Hair picked up the mite from his robes, still asleep, and laid him over his shoulder. Then, with Little Horse and Two Twists supporting Touch the Sky, the group headed for the sick lodge.

It was the longest walk Touch the Sky could ever remember making. He could not tell, in this early-morning stillness, what the word was. It was quiet around the sick lodge, a small structure made from skins stretched over a frame of bent poles.

Touch the Sky paused with one hand gripping the buffalo-hide entrance flap. For a moment, all strength deserted him. He had faced down bullet, bow, and grizzly. But if Honey Eater had crossed over, Touch the Sky was not sure he was strong enough to endure the blow.

"H'ar now," Knobby said with false gruffness,

for in fact the old man was on the verge of tears himself. "Toss that flap back like the man you are, Matthew, and grasp the nettle!"

But at that moment, the decision was taken out of the young Cheyenne's hands.

"Will you men wake up the entire camp?" came a weak but recognizable voice from within, scolding them. "I can hear you in here! Will someone feed a hungry woman?"

With a shout of joy, Touch the Sky limped inside, the rest on his heels. Honey Eater lay propped up in a pile of robes, Sharp Nosed Woman at her side, tears of joy streaming down her face.

For a long moment, Touch the Sky and Honey Eater exchanged a glance—one whose meaning had become familiar for them. A glance that said: *Once again we have defeated the Black Warrior.* Then he was kneeling at her side, placing the sleeping Little Bear with her.

Sharp Nosed Woman had been casting suspicious glances at Old Knobby. But when he pointed at her and made the blossom sign—telling her she was as pretty as a flower—she blushed.

"Now you have all seen her," Sharp Nosed Woman fussed. "And you see she is still a pretty one. Now go, bring her a tender elk steak! I want it dripping in marrow fat, do you hear?"

It was understood that women were the masters in the sick lodge, and no brave ever took offense at being ordered about like a child if it was for the welfare of the sick and wounded. Even a chief could be put to work if an old grandmother demanded it from the lodge. Touch the Sky cleared out at Sharp Nosed Woman's command, though Little Bear was permitted to stay.

Immediately, seeing the joy in Touch the Sky's face, the camp crier began his rounds, shouting the news that Honey Eater had survived. Many, still half asleep, nonetheless came outside to sing the song to the new sun rising, joyous at her recovery.

"The Holy Ones smiled on you, buck," Little Horse told his friend as they prepared Honey Eater's meal. They knew she had lost much blood, so they also made a nourishing soup of calf brains and rose hips.

"They did," Touch the Sky agreed. In truth he was letting his friend do most of the work, for he was still too sore and weak from his overnight vigil. "But what Big Tree did cannot—*will* not—stand."

Little Horse nodded. "As you say. Our Medicine Arrows are still stained with dirty blood from Sis-ki-dee's murder of he who may not be mentioned."

Little Horse meant their former peace chief, Gray Thunder. By custom his name could not be spoken, for it was believed the dead might hear it and answer.

"This time," Little Horse continued, "the renegades were not content to shoot at us from afar, as Sis-ki-dee did when he killed our chief. Never mind that it was your woman. They violated our very camp itself!"

"You have seized this matter firmly by the tail," Touch the Sky said. "They are like daring children testing their elders. If this crime goes unavenged, they will be even more emboldened."

Besides all that, Touch the Sky thought, Big Tree hurt the Cheyenne's best reason for living. Now the Comanche would die a hard death. Touch the Sky had failed to kill Sis-ki-dee in Bloody Bones Canyon. That failure, in part, had encouraged Big Tree's bold attack. There could be no failure this time.

When Big Tree set out from Lookout Rock, he took five good ponies on his string.

White men divided time up into odd things called hours and minutes and seconds. But Big Tree knew that time was a bird, and now that bird was on the wing.

Touch the Sky, being a "noble red man," would remain in camp so long as his woman's life lay in the balance. But once she died—and she might already be dead—the tall one would move like wings of swift lightning.

So Big Tree rode his ponies hard, rode them right into the ground. He would hold one at a full, or near, gallop until it lathered, then switch to another at full speed. These moves were effortless for a Comanche, a tribe who were ungainly on foot but gracious as eagles in flight when on horseback.

He had stuffed his legging sash with jerked buffalo and dried fruit and did not need to stop to hunt or prepare food. Steadily south he fled, leaving the brown, rolling plains of the north behind him as he entered the sandstone country of the southern Colorado Territory. Deeper, through the opening whites called Raton Pass, into the land of the Pueblo tribes and the scant-grass deserts.

Big Tree had run his horses ragged by the time he reached Navajo country. The southwest tribes were rich in horses this year, so it was an easy matter to steal a new string. Deeper he fled, through the desolate no-man's-land of the Staked Plain, across the great alkali pan of southern New Mexico.

Deeper, across the wide, shallow, muddy-brown river whites called the Rio Grande, Mexicans the Río Bravo. Deeper, always deeper, for he knew the tall one would be coming. It had finally come down to this time and this country.

For many winters now the two of them had played their deadly game of cat and mouse. Now the playing was over. Now one of them would die, and it would be a hard death.

Touch the Sky knew he could count on the moccasin telegraph to track Big Tree's movements even before he left camp. The brave did not ride out for several sleeps, for he knew better than to track Big Tree when his strength was down.

Smoke signals, mirror flashes, runners—every means was used as each tribe let the others know what this important and deadly renegade was up to. Touch the Sky was not surprised to learn that, as he expected, Big Tree had fled due south at a breakneck pace.

"He means to hole up in the Blanco Canyon," the tall brave informed his band. Knobby, too, sat around the fire, for he had been invited to remain in camp until Touch the Sky rode out. That way the two friends could ride together as far as Big-horn Falls.

"He can be flushed," Two Twists said confidently. None of Touch the Sky's companions had mounted a serious argument when Touch the Sky announced he was going after Big Tree alone. They understood that the real danger lay right here in camp. With Touch the Sky gone, Wolf Who Hunts Smiling and his lickspittles could rebel at any moment.

"Our shaman knows that canyon," Little Horse agreed. "If any of us can trap Big Tree in his own burrow, it is Touch the Sky."

And so the brave set out. He cleaned and oiled his Sharps and crimped a pouch full of shells; he made a new bow of green oak and strung it with tough buffalo sinew; he filled his foxskin quiver with new, fire-hardened arrows. He selected his favorite coyote dun and three other ponies; then, Old Knobby at his side, he rode out for the south country.

It was during this leg of the journey, the stretch between Powder River and Bighorn Falls, that Touch the Sky learned some disturbing news through the moccasin telegraph.

He and Knobby were just clearing the last series of razorback ridges north of Bighorn Falls when Touch the Sky saw smoke lines rising on the southern horizon: a message from the Southern Cheyenne camp at Washita Creek.

"Heap big doin's down south," Knobby observed, craning his withered neck to watch the dark puffs rise against a seamless blue sky the color of a gas flame. "What're they sayin', colt?"

A deep frown settled over Touch the Sky's weather-rawed features. "Big Tree did not hole up in the Blanco. He has fled into Old Mexico."

This was troubling news. Touch the Sky had counted on familiarity with the Blanco Canyon country to work in his favor. Big Tree was a formidable opponent on any battleground. But to fight him in new country was a daunting prospect—and whereas Big Tree was intimate with Mexico, Touch the Sky had never once crossed the border.

"He has allies there," the Cheyenne said glumly. "He is fluent in the tongue, knows the country like beavers know the timberline. It is a good choice on his part. And as for me, I have no choice but to follow him there."

"Well, I reckon that tears it," Knobby announced. "Looks like you 'n' me'll be ridin' together agin'. Just like when we whipped ol' Wes Munro and his land-grabbers."

Touch the Sky squinted at him. "You been chewing peyote, old codger?"

"You're the one what's soft in the brain," the trapper retorted, "iffen you think you kin just waltz into beaner country and flush Big Tree! *Puedes entenderme ahora?*"

At Touch the Sky's puzzled glance, the old man translated, "I just asked you in Mexer talk iffen you kin savvy what I said. I spent damn near five years with the Taos Trappers, learned Mexer talk real good. I made three, four pack-train runs down the King's Highway, too, between Santa Fe and Durango, Mexico. I may be all tied up with the rheumatick, boy. But I can still make my beaver. C'mon, Matthew, wha'd'ya say, boy? I can send a note to your ma and pa by a runner, tell 'em I got unexpected business down to the south country. It won't even be a lie."

Touch the Sky did not really debate it very long. He was an equal match for Big Tree, but not under unequal terms. Old Knobby was right—the savvy old mountain man might be slower in body these days, but his mind was sharp as a steel trap. This old frontiersman had taught Touch the Sky everything he knew about nighttime movement and survival, among other things. He'd be a good companion on this daunting mission.

"Good chance you might get killed," he warned the old-timer.

"Damn right," Knobby replied happily, chucking up his horse. "Wouldn't be no fun otherwise."

Chapter Five

In the hardscrabble years following the war with the United States in 1846–47, Old Mexico had become a country laid waste by road bandits and raiding Indians. The corruption of Santa Anna and other so-called generals had left the Mexican Army with beautiful uniforms, but demoralized, corrupt, and woefully inadequate to protect the vast frontier. Ambitious *jefes*, or "bosses," formed their own private armies and roamed virtually unchallenged—until another gang of thieves clashed with them over control of a region.

No *jefe* ruled with such total control, or inspired as much total fear, as the cruel Pablo Morales, known to friend and foe alike as Poco Loco because he was indeed "a little crazy."

Poco Loco and his gang of ten *pistoleros* ruled northern Sonora state. They operated out of a remote mountain bastion, the "lost pueblo" of Santa Rosa high in the snowcapped sierras. With Santa Rosa as a base, they struck with impunity at government caravans, private pack trains, border-survey teams, anything that moved along the nearly deserted roads.

Between raids, Poco Loco made his headquarters in Santa Rosa's only cantina, a little adobe hovel called Las Tres Hermanas, The Three Sisters. Normally it was dead as last Christmas in the cantina, especially since all locals knew who holed up there and either stayed away or behaved very carefully indeed when they went in. Pablo Morales was not always mean, and could in fact be quite generous when Captain Whiskey had him in tow. But like a half-wild mustang, he was totally unpredictable, and in an eyeblink could kill a man for snoring.

But on this night, his mood was jolly. A party of *ciboleros*, Mexican buffalo hunters, was passing through from Chihuahua. They brought the latest gossip from the Internal Provinces, and were quite diverting. The hunters knew of Poco Loco only by reputation, not sight, and did not hesitate when the squat, serape-draped, free-spending stranger challenged them to an arm-wrestling contest.

Most of Poco Loco's men were hanging around in the cantina, nursing bottles of tequila and forty-rod, and placed bets on their *jefe*. One by one, Poco Loco defeated the young, strong hunters. After four hard matches, he had not even broken a sweat.

"Amigo," said the leader of the *ciboleros* at one point, pointing to a man sprawled in the back corner. "That man there, he has been asleep for hours. Should someone wake him and send him home? His wife will worry all night."

Several of Poco Loco's men laughed outright.

"You hear this, 'manos?" Poco Loco's man Esteban shouted to the rest. "Wake Senor Ramirez up and send him home to his woman!"

This occasioned another roar of laughter.

Poco Loco, still busy pocketing his winnings, looked up at the hunter, his cruel mouth tilting into a grin. The broad, bluff face was dusky with beard stubble, and a livid scar ran from his left temple down below the point of his jaw. A sawed-off scattergun hung in a special rig at his side.

"Friend," Poco Loco told the hunter, "that man has gone home permanently. I killed him several hours ago. You see, he was angry at me. Something about his sister and the loss of her honor."

The hunter traded uncomfortable glances with his companions.

"Shouldn't someone at least drag him out?" the leader asked hesitantly.

Poco Loco shrugged beefy shoulders under his serape. "Right now he is only drawing flies. Drag him out when he begins to stink."

The *ciboleros* finally realized who the strong stranger was. They left shortly after this, thanking Jesus for sparing them. But before long the batwings sprang open again and a huge figure moved into the cantina. A wide-brimmed plainsman's hat was pulled low, leaving his face in shadow in the dark interior. He ordered a cup of the local wine, then turned to the rest.

"Tengo cien dolares en oro," he announced. "I

have one hundred dollars in gold. My money says I can whip the king of the arm wrestlers."

Absolute silence greeted these words. Esteban and the rest watched, hands inching toward their weapons, as the huge stranger moved closer. His boot heels thumped on the floor, and the canny Poco Loco noticed that he walked as one unused to wearing shoe leather.

Poco Loco watched him, his swarthy face impassive, while he poured himself another shot of tequila. "Put your gold on the table, stranger," he invited.

The new arrival stacked ten American quarter eagles before the Mexican. Then he scraped a chair close, sat down, rolled up his sleeve. Still his face was obscured by shadow and the dim light from a single argand lamp. Poco Loco stared closer, recognizing that mocking grin.

"Just to make things interesting," the challenger said, placing an old coffee can on the table. He drew out two scorpions, handling them carefully, and placed them on their backs on the table, the deadly tails pointing up.

He arranged them so that the hand of whoever lost would come down right on top of one of them.

A buzz of excited talk swept through the cantina. Poco Loco's men gathered closer. The Mexican *jefe* grinned, revealing yellow teeth like two rows of crooked gravestones.

"This stranger," he said to his men. "I like him. He has a set on him. Maybe this one will live."

The two men gripped each other's hand and commenced their struggle. First Poco Loco started to win, then the challenger. The veins in their necks stood out like fat night crawlers, their muscles strained like taut cables.

The stranger gave a mighty shout, and then there was a loud thump as Poco Loco's hand smashed to the table, right on top of one of the scorpions, so hard the insect was instantly crushed.

Esteban's gun was halfway out of its holster when Poco Loco called out, "Lower your hammer, Esteban, and look closer! He pulled the stingers out of their tails. This is an old *compadre* of ours."

Big Tree whipped the hat aside. At the same time, he slid the gold across to his old friend.

"Keep it," he said. "Consider it your first payment."

Poco Loco had in fact already recognized Big Tree—one of the few men strong enough to beat him at arm wrestling. They had shared a virtual reign of terror many years earlier, before the Comanche moved on to the north country.

Gold was extremely rare in Mexico. Poco Loco stared at the coins, and his tongue brushed across his upper lip.

"The first payment on what?" he demanded.

"On the head of a Northern Cheyenne named Touch the Sky," Big Tree answered. "Also known as Matthew Hanchon of Bighorn Falls in the Wyoming Territory."

It was true that there was a reward on Touch the Sky's head. Years before, Hiram Steele had announced that he would pay three thousand in gold, no questions asked, to the man who could deliver him the head of Matthew Hanchon. That offer still stood.

"Wyoming?" Poco Loco asked. "Big Tree, I never knew you for a fool. That is thousands of miles from here. You know me, red one. I have made too many gringo enemies. I will not cross the border—the Americans have a better record of tracking down their outlaws."

"You will need to go nowhere," the renegade assured him. "Hanchon is coming to us."

"Why?"

Big Tree grinned. "I tried to stab him. I missed. I hit his woman instead. He is a 'noble' warrior who will never let this crime stand. He is coming to kill me."

"And you fear him?" Poco Loco said incredulously. "You? One of the few men I consider an equal?"

"I fear him," Big Tree admitted. "And I feel no shame admitting it. This is the warrior who killed Iron Eyes."

This news forced new respect from Poco Loco. Iron Eyes, once Big Tree's bosom companion in crime, had been the leader of the Kaitsenko—the most elite group of Kiowa warriors.

Poco Loco nodded. "You are right to fear him, and only a fool would not. But, Big Tree, it takes an even bigger fool to come into Sonora with blood in his eyes."

Poco Loco glanced toward the dead man in the corner, then at the room full of well-armed, battle-scarred hard cases. "How many men is he bringing with him?" he demanded.

"He is alone."

Poco Loco poured out a shot for Big Tree. "That is sad indeed, for no man should die alone."

* * *

"There she is, sprout," Old Knobby announced as the two riders topped a low bluff. "The Río Bravo. Look at her. Damn near four hundred yards across right here, but she won't wet the horses' knees."

The great river marking the international border wound through the valley below them, creating narrow green strips of growth in the vast, arid expanse surrounding them.

"Watch," said Knobby as they let their horses set their own pace toward the water. "She looks muddy brown from here, but that water'll be clear as spring runoff when we're close."

He was right, Touch the Sky noticed. The water was so clear, and the current so slow, you could almost miss it when your face was close. Both men threw their bridles, Knobby loosing the claybank's girth, before they let the tired, hot mounts plunge their noses into the river.

Both men flopped onto their bellies and drank, then plunged their heads into the water. Touch the Sky shook his eyes clear and made a careful check in all directions. Even up north it was common news that Mexico, exasperated by Indian raids into their country from the United States, had stepped up patrols along the border. And they were dealing summarily with any illegals caught in their country—especially red illegals, for no one despised Indians more than the Mexicans.

Knobby, too, scouted the terrain as he gnawed on a strip of jerked buffalo. The hard pace showed around his haggard eyes, and the old-timer mounted and dismounted with noticeable grunts.

But Touch the Sky had been impressed with Knobby's trail skills and still-sharp senses.

"See anything?" Knobby demanded.

"Dust puffs," Touch the Sky said. "South by southeast. Still too far away to tell anything, though. Could be a herd of antelope."

"Could be," Knobby agreed. "But we had us a smooth trip down. Too smooth. Trouble never leaves either one of us alone that long. Get set for more, you red son of the plains."

Touch the Sky's shaman sense—a slight prickling in his nape—told him the same thing. But there was nothing else for it: They must ride toward those puffs. All signs and all reports pointed in that direction, for it was the path taken by Big Tree.

They rested briefly, mainly to let the horses graze the grass near the river. Knobby had told Touch the Sky that graze would soon be scarce to nonexistent. For this reason, the two men had swapped two steel knives and a fine buffalo robe for two sacks of corn at a Navajo village near Winrock. It would be rationed sparingly to their mounts.

An hour south of the Río Bravo, Knobby halted them and broke out his brass Cavalry binoculars. After studying the dust puffs for a full minute, he announced, "God-in-whirlwinds, boy! Here comes the fight! It's *federales*, I can tell from the brass plates on their kepis. Mebbe fifty of 'em, and they've got us in their sights! They'll be in range quicker 'n scat. We best pull foot."

"Hold on," Touch the Sky said. "You're the one

who always told me it's best to take trouble by the horns."

Knobby removed his flap hat and scratched the bald hide at his pate. "Fifty agin two? You damn Cheyennes have got fightin' fettle, I'll give you that any day. But, pup, they'll cut us to stew meat! A Mexer is a poor shot, but look around. We got no cover here."

"Won't need it," Touch the Sky insisted, pulling his Sharps out of its boot. "Doctor me up some cartridges, old coot. Buffalo loads. I want double loads of black powder, at least two hundred grains per load."

Knobby caught on instantly when his companion said buffalo loads. Even as the old trapper began to uncrimp some cartridges, he said, "Double load will give you range, for sure. But you'll lose accuracy. Raise your muzzle. I'll try to spot your shots."

Touch the Sky prepared his Sharps, loading one of the double-charged shots and placing a primer cap on the nib behind the hammer. Then he hastily leveled a spot in the sand and took up a prone position, laying his muzzle across a low, flat rock to steady it.

He sighted down the barrel toward the advancing dust puffs and fired.

"Good range!" Knobby shouted behind him. "But you got windage drift to your left."

Touch the Sky reloaded and adjusted his muzzle angle. At his next shot, Knobby loosed a whoop.

"*That*'ll learn the stupid sons a bitches to cluster up!" the old-timer gloated. "You dropped a horse,

Matthew! That's holdin' 'n' squeezin', boy!"

Several more shots did it. The advancing party, still stuck out of effective range of their weapons, would not risk death in this open terrain. They veered due east.

"You done 'er, Matthew," Knobby said as they secured their gear to resume the trek. "But that red devil Big Tree won't rabbit as easy as them federals just done."

"I hope you're right, old friend," Touch the Sky replied. "I didn't come down here to make Big Tree run. I came down here to kill him."

Chapter Six

Captain Salvador de la Fuentes was worried.

He rode at the head of two small columns of dragoons and lancers. Between the columns, each made up of ten soldiers, rumbled a big Mexican-made freight wagon known as a wheeled tarantula. The civilian teamster glanced all around them, sweat pouring from under his straw Sonora.

Captain de la Fuentes could not blame the driver for his nervous fidgeting. To their left rose the sawtooth peaks of the sierra known as the Bad Death Mountains. On their right was a series of basalt turrets, each capable of hiding a rider.

And the whole world knew that this was Poco Loco's territory.

It was hard enough duty, being stuck for years at a time at a godforsaken frontier outpost, chasing the shadows of Indians and fighting dysentery and boredom. But these road bandits . . . well, at least this time the military supply wagon was well-protected, the captain reminded himself. Double the usual number of men. And his lancers were the pride of the Mexican Army, having proved themselves again and again in hard campaigns against a tough American army. Any of them would die before they would retreat, never mind the odds.

They were coming to the worst stretch, a sandy wash that made it difficult for the horses to run.

De la Fuentes slewed around in his saddle and raised his fist. "Take up wide intervals!" he shouted down the line to his *teniente*. "Dragoons, fix bayonets!"

The officer eased his heavy French revolver from its stiff holster and laid it on his right thigh at the ready.

"Maldito!" Esteban cursed. "They have doubled their manpower, *jefe*. And look! Lancers. No men to fool with."

Poco Loco took the glasses from his lackey and studied the formation below. He, Esteban, and Big Tree were crouched behind a basalt formation. The rest of Poco Loco's men were spaced about them behind other formations.

"It looks bad," the bandit leader agreed. "I have never been one to earn my breakfast if I can get it by some easy way. This is no easy way. We had better let it be this time."

Big Tree, a mocking grin playing at his lips, didn't bother taking the glasses. "Amigo, you have lost your fire! Time was, you would drive Texas Rangers out of breastworks just for sport! But never mind. I will make it easy for you to steal your breakfast. Watch me, and see how a Comanche can take the fight to an enemy!"

Big Tree stripped his cayuse of all rigging, leaving his rifle with Poco Loco. He took only his osage-wood bow and two quivers stuffed with arrows. And what he did next left the Mexican thieves struck dumb with wonder.

The soldiers saw Big Tree approaching, his pony running a defensive zigzag pattern, while he was still out of easy range. Bouncing freely on the back of his galloping pony, holding on only with his powerful legs, the renegade grabbed a handful of arrows and strung them so fast that no one could count the shots.

His first lightning volley dropped horses and caused shrieks of human and animal pain. The lancers formed a skirmish line and charged. Big Tree dropped them like clay targets, not discriminating between man and horse.

This still left him one full quiver. By the time that, too, was emptied into the main formation, Poco Loco knew the odds were in his favor.

The battle was brief, more of a massacre than a fight. Poco Loco himself killed the officer, using his shotgun to turn the man's face into a red smear as the soldier lay wounded on the ground. Esteban went around to all the bodies, putting a finishing shot in each man's brain.

"Big Tree," Poco Loco declared, "having you around is like having a second gang."

However, his jubilation was short-lived, for the

pickings turned out to be slim. Yes, they could certainly use the food and coffee, as well as the medical supplies. But this shipment included no payroll cash and no liquor rations—the real reason for the strike.

Poco Loco stared at all the dead men, sprawled just as they had fallen. Soon the carrion birds would be picking their bones clean.

"This is the way it is," he complained to Big Tree. "I strike, I kill, I go away with spider leavings for my trouble. I need gold. Are you sure this noble Cheyenne is coming? This red man whose plew is worth three thousand?"

Big Tree was a long time answering. He studied the shimmering haze over the sierra, then looked at his old companion. "Am I sure he is coming? No, mad one. I am sure he is *here*."

After diverting the advancing *federales*, Touch the Sky and Old Knobby veered to the southwest, keeping the Río Bravo always over their right shoulders. Through a combination of trail signs and careful questioning, they had determined Big Tree's general direction.

But there were many possible strongholds here at the vast frontier dividing the two young nations. Reaching some of them would entail laborious climbs up steep headlands, time-consuming treks through countless canyons.

"The moccasin telegraph does not end at the border," Touch the Sky told Knobby. "It can't because the tribes don't end. Which Indians live around here besides the Kiowas and Comanches and Navajos?"

"Papagos," Knobby said. "Some Pimas, Tewas, Yaquis. Some of 'em is Pueblo peoples, others've come up from the jungles down in Mex or even farther down, way the hell down."

Touch the Sky had heard of these tribes, but never met any of them. But Knobby had already told him, in the long hours they spent in the saddle and in camp at night, something about these southern tribes. Most of them were not as warlike as the northern tribes, and riding in this blazing sun, Touch the Sky could understand that. The year-round heat down here sapped a man of his fighting fettle.

He soon had his chance to meet a Mexican tribe. Toward midday on their third day past the border, the two friends rose up out of a long, deep arroyo. Before them sprawled an unwalled complex of adobe huts, crude pole corrals, and neatly cultivated fields irrigated with an *acequia madre*, or mother ditch, run off the nearby Río Bravo.

"Papago village," Knobby announced, pointing to the fine horseflesh in a corral. "The Papagos're natural-born horsemen, damn near as good as a Comanche."

"They friendly?" Touch the Sky asked.

"I wouldn't 'xactly say that. Cortez and the rest of them fish-eaters have left 'em leery of visitors, if you catch my drift. But they live and let live. We should be safe riding in under the peace sign."

Knobby was right. Several sun-coppered Indians working in the fields watched the two men suspiciously as they approached a group of men conferring over a broken wagon wheel they were repairing.

Judd Cole

Knobby greeted them in Spanish, and they nodded, greeting him back. Though the two men were not invited to dismount, a goatskin of cool well water was passed up to them. Both men drank. The Papagos looked curiously at Touch the Sky while he watched them. They were especially fascinated by the enemy scalps hanging from his sash. A few had obviously come from white men.

"Ask them," Touch the Sky told Knobby, "if they have heard anything about a stranger riding into this area. A big, fearsome Comanche. The one who commands the Wendigo Mountain stronghold."

Knobby spoke in rapid Spanish. The men seemed to understand him, but no one offered to speak.

"Tell them," Touch the Sky said, "that he is a murderer of women and children. Tell them he shoved cold steel into my woman's vitals. Tell them he has come to their land to kill their women and children. Tell them I have come from the land of the short white days, all this way to kill him. To make sure he never hurts another woman or child."

The Papagos were silent for a long time after Knobby translated all this, watching Touch the Sky. Finally, one of them spoke to Knobby. When he finished, the old trailsman turned to Touch the Sky.

"This one says they have nothing to go on but your word. But he says he has looked deep into your eyes and seen the soul of an honorable man. He believes you. He also tells me you have strong medicine, and that if he defies it, bad dreams will be placed over his eyes. He asked if you are called a shaman."

Touch the Sky met the man's eyes and nodded.

"He says," Knobby continued, "that the man you want is said to be in Santa Rosa. That's ten miles past here, a little *pueblito* way the hell up a mountainside. Says Big Tree has thrown in with a hardcase *jefe* by the name of Poco Loco."

Touch the Sky nodded again. He reached into his pannier, drew out a pouch filled with rich white man's tobacco, and gave it to the Indian who had spoken. Before they rode off, the man added something else.

"What'd he say?" Touch the Sky asked.

Knobby scowled. "Said to tell you, best cover your ass. The *gobernador* of Sonora has offered a two-hundred-peso bounty on the scalps of wild Indians. That's how come these is all wearin' their hair so short—so's scalpers can't get holt of it."

"I appreciate the warning," Touch the Sky said. "Maybe I'll even cut my hair. But for right now, let's make tracks toward Santa Rosa. I want to get the lay of the place. Then I mean to strike right off. We have to let Big Tree know, right from the jump, that he's got no place to hide. And that goes for anybody who tries to help him."

Poco Loco's mood improved considerably as the day advanced and the level in his tequila bottle steadily went down.

"I say it now, compadres," he called out to his men, most of whom surrounded him at the little deal tables of the Three Sisters cantina. "We did not become rich men today. But did you see this red killing machine? *Qué destreza!* What skill in the killing arts! Big Tree, I have seen the gringo circus in Texas. Their trick shooters on trained ponies could not stand in your shadow."

Big Tree nodded slightly, acknowledging the praise. But he kept a careful eye on Poco Loco. The man was like the Spaniards—one hand extended in friendship while the other always hid a knife.

However, the canny renegade had indeed figured one thing right: Poco Loco might be treacherous, but he was also cunning. Big Tree wanted him to appreciate his warrior skills—which were also, of course, a bandit's skills. If Poco Loco thought Big Tree might make him rich, he would protect him like the Virgin Mary.

And protection was what Big Tree needed. He was sure, deep down in his bone marrow, that Touch the Sky was out there. Right now. Watching, waiting, biding his time until the perfect moment. Big Tree could kill him, but he must buy time.

A sudden scuffling of chairs, and abrupt female shrieking, made both men look toward the back corner. Esteban and several of the men had been drinking heavily since the raid on the army supply caravan. A flash of snow-white skin and red-lace petticoat told them what was happening to the young woman who served tables.

Poco Loco shouted to get their attention. "Esteban, I have told you before, this building was once a chapel. None of that inside. Take her out into the courtyard."

Big Tree grinned as the men dragged the protesting woman outside. "No one can say you lack a sense of propriety, my friend."

Poco Loco grinned. "There is very little I—we— will lack, my Comanche friend, once I unleash you on the Camino Real. Some of the merchant trains bound for Durango and Aguascalientes have only five or six private guards. However, it takes money to make money. My men need weapons, new rigs, liquor. I am starting to believe you are waiting for a chimera. You said this Cheyenne is already among us, but what? Is he like God himself, everywhere felt but nowhere seen? I have neither seen him nor felt his presence."

Big Tree was about to reply when a sound like a shriek of the damned made both men flinch. Poco Loco even dropped his glass into his lap.

The hell-spawned scream was followed, after a brief, shocked silence, by a mad confusion of shouts and curses.

"Amigo," Big Tree said calmly. "You have not yet seen him, and it will be some time before you do. But one of your men has just felt him."

Poco Loco pushed away from the table and stumbled outside. Big Tree, still grinning, followed more slowly. He was not surprised by what they found.

A man, his trousers still tangled around his legs, lay dead in the *plaza mayor*, or main square. An arrow slanted at a forty-five-degree angle through his head, having entered behind the right ear and exited through the left eye socket.

"Look, Poco Loco," Big Tree called out merrily. "The arrow is fletched with crow feathers. Only one tribe fletches with crow feathers. Guess which

Judd Cole

tribe that is. And now some advice. Cover down, if you value life itself. From now on, keep a wall behind you and a tree on both sides."

Big Tree glanced up toward the grainy darkness of the mountains surrounding them. Then he looked at Poco Loco and noticed that the hardened killer was shocked sober.

"More will die," Big Tree said. "But we can kill him. And the gold for his head will outfit us for the King's Highway and a life of riches."

"We can kill him," Poco Loco agreed. "And we will. But much slower than Francisco here died. I will bury him under the sun up to his neck and then slice off his eyelids. An eye for an eye. Only then will your Senor Hiram Steele get the head."

Chapter Seven

"Look at them," Medicine Flute gloated, nodding across the wide central clearing. "Keeping vigil for their noble red man."

Wolf Who Hunts Smiling and the rest of the Bullwhips, gathered in a council circle just outside Medicine Flute's tipi, nodded at these words. But in fact, many of the people around Touch the Sky's tipi were merely visitors coming with little presents for Honey Eater and her child.

"With luck," Wolf Who Hunts Smiling chipped in, "their long vigil will finally be rewarded by the return of his bones. If I have reckoned Big Tree right, this time White Man Runs Him is riding to the last battle."

"I could only wish," Medicine Flute said, "that he might have suffered the agony of seeing his woman die before him."

"Never mind her," said Crow Killer, leader of the Bullwhip Soldiers. "We will have a free hand with her and their whelp after the tall one is gone under. I mean to take her out on the prairie."

Crow Killer was referring to the ancient custom frowned upon by many. Men in authority could declare a woman tainted and "take her out on the prairie"—that is, any man who wanted to was welcome to top her. After this, the shamed woman always killed herself, for there could be no place for her in the tribe. And an Indian without a tribe was a dead Indian.

"Look there," Wolf Who Hunts Smiling said. "Here comes Two Twists again, anxious to report the latest news about Touch the Sky learned from the moccasin telegraph. See? Even now he is running over to Little Horse with it. You can see from the glad light in his face that the tall one still has breath in his nostrils."

"Patience, Panther Clan," Crow Killer cautioned the Wolf. "Killing Touch the Sky will take time. How long have all of us been trying? How many times have we failed? Big Tree can do it, but give him some time."

Medicine Flute had been mulling something while the rest talked. Suddenly a canny glow came into his eyes. He had been absently blowing on his leg-bone flute while he thought. Now he laid his instrument aside and addressed the others.

"Brothers! Have ears. I am keen for a little sport. Why wait for Big Tree? How would you enjoy watching Honey Eater's face, not to mention the faces of Touch the Sky's men, when they learn he has been killed? And even better, how would you like to convince Touch the Sky, before he dies in the south country, that his woman is dead?"

Wolf Who Hunts Smiling frowned impatiently. "What, are we girls playing let's pretend in our sewing lodge? I call you shaman only to fool the fools, bone blower. Have you grown to believe in your own false magic?"

"Magic?" Medicine Flute scoffed. "Add magic to an empty gun, and you are a dead man. Never mind magic, Panther Clan. Only think. How do our enemies get their news about their noble champion?"

Wolf Who Hunts Smiling was impatient, with a hair-trigger temper. But he was also wily and quick. Almost immediately after Medicine Flute's question, the Wolf's lupine grin spread across his face.

"Of course," he said softly. "The moccasin telegraph."

Medicine Flute's fleshy lips formed a triumphant smirk. "As you say, buck. Crow Killer can pick one of his best soldiers. He can tell the Headmen he needs to send the man out for an extended scout. That man rides deep into the south country. Once there, he sends up false smoke."

"And false smoke blows both ways," Wolf Who Hunts Smiling said. "Our man down south sends up word of Touch the Sky's death. Meantime, up here, we send up smoke saying that Honey Eater died from her wound after all. And truly, she had not come sassy yet before he left. There is often a fatal fever after a false healing."

This was indeed a stroke of genius, and the rest congratulated Medicine Flute for his inventiveness. As for Wolf Who Hunts Smiling, in his secret heart of hearts, he was not at all convinced that Big Tree could indeed kill Touch the Sky. But something like this could. In his agony, Touch the Sky would lose focus, would let the red-hot emotions govern the cold killer. And against a foe like Big Tree, one mistake was all it took to send a man to sleep with the worms.

"Pick a good man," the Wolf ordered Crow Killer. "Tell him to take a good string of horses with him and to ride hard. Send him to my lodge before he rides out. I want to be sure he has the message right. Big Tree's knife did not kill Honey Eater. But we will watch her die inside when she hears her bull has been felled."

"As you say," Medicine Flute agreed. "And when our false smoke about her death blows south, the misery you see in her face will be reflected in his."

Touch the Sky and Knobby had made a fairly dry, if somewhat cool, camp in a cave high in the mountains above Santa Rosa. From the mouth of the cave, they could see the little pueblo spread out below in a teacup-shaped hollow. The night before, Touch the Sky had crawled down about five hundred feet from the cave to launch the deadly shot that killed one of Big Tree's companions.

Knowing their survival depended on staying in motion, the two friends had quit the cave the very next morning, moving to a well-hidden cleft in the caprock. Sure enough, Big Tree and one of the Mexicans—a bear of a man with a livid scar covering half of his face—had come searching the area and located the cave.

"I could draw a bead on them now," Touch the Sky said almost wishfully, watching them from behind a shoulder of lava rock.

"You could," Knobby agreed. "And then we'd be gone beaver on account it's flush of day and there ain't nothin' behind us but cliffs. They'd come up here to flush us, sure as hell's afire."

Reluctantly, Touch the Sky nodded. It was good to hold the high ground, but not when you had no escape trail. Besides, he wanted to make Big Tree sweat a little. A quick kill would let him off too light. He needed to see death happening all around him, closing in on him. Touch the Sky wanted him to suffer from night sweats, frazzled nerves, the kind of pressure that drove a man mad with worry. Only then would he grant him the dog's death he deserved.

Tell me how you die, Arrow Keeper had once said, *and I will tell you what you're worth.*

"Well begun is half done," Knobby assured his young companion. "That kill last night, Matthew, was a good start. But they're forted up down there. That must be Poco Loco with Big Tree, and he looks about half rough. Plus look at them houses— loopholed for rifles. Ten men could hold off a regiment. What we got to do, we got to make it hot for 'em around here. We got to make 'em break and run. We get 'em in a running fight, we got mebbe half a chance."

Touch the Sky nodded, watching the two men below as they began to return to Santa Rosa.

"You're right, old trooper. We have to make it

hot for them. Too hot to hang around here. We can't rush that town, but we can sure as hell sneak in after dark. We're going to pay Big Tree and his Mexican friends a friendly little visit tonight."

The night after Francisco's head was skewered by an arrow, the streets and plaza of Santa Rosa were deserted.

The local citizens, long subjugated by cutthroats and tyrants, knew only that yet another battle was being waged with their town as the site. They were used to staying indoors after darkness anyway, to avoid the depredations of Poco Loco's drunken men.

Poco Loco, however, fumed at the humiliation of being locked down in his own stronghold. He had the windows of the Three Sisters cantina reinforced with stout boards and posted sentries on the rooftops of the town.

"I am glad to see you, 'mano," Poco Loco informed Big Tree over a hand of faro. "Truly glad you have returned to the country where we notched our first kills. But you have brought a smallpox blanket back with you in this Cheyenne cur."

Big Tree tossed down a card. "I spent much of this day looking for sign. I found very little. But we must continue to try flushing him out by day. That, and maintain absolute vigilance by night."

Even as Big Tree fell silent, one of the sentries called out the all clear. The rest followed suit.

"Full moon tonight," Poco Loco remarked. "And up here in the mountains, every night is brilliant with stars. Also, I have told my men to keep brush fires burning at both ends of the town. A mouse would have trouble entering this town unobserved."

Big Tree said nothing to this, only sliding his big, steel-framed .44 from its holster and checking the loads. Watching him, Poco Loco nervously slid his sawed-off scattergun from its hip sling and laid it across the table.

"You think he will sneak in anyway?" Poco Loco asked.

Big Tree thumbed his hammer to half-cock. "Do I think he *will*? No. I think he is already here."

A harsh bark of laughter was Poco Loco's only response. But in the long, unbroken silence that followed, the big Mexican's face began to sweat.

He glanced around the dimly lighted interior. The old man who owned the place cowered behind the short plank counter, wishing they would go away. An old local, almost toothless, sat nursing a bowl of beans and tortillas in the back corner. With men on sentry duty, the place was almost deserted.

Outside, an owl hooted. Slowly, Big Tree let his chair settle forward onto its front legs. Poco Loco watched his face.

"What?" the Mexican demanded. "It was only an owl."

"Was it, crazy one? And how many owls have you noticed making their nests up here in the mountains instead of down in the forested valleys?"

Poco Loco said nothing. Outside, the owl hoot sounded again, but it seemed to have moved slightly.

"Should we go outside?" he asked Big Tree.

The Comanche shook his head. "No need to go looking for your own grave."

Slowly, methodically, with the infinite patience of a warrior focused on nothing but victory, Touch the Sky made his way carefully down the side of the mountain.

He had left Knobby to the important task of caring for their ponies, which were hidden in a grassy barranca perhaps a mile across the nearest ridge. Touch the Sky had stripped down to his clout and his moccasins, taking no weapon but his obsidian knife.

The moonlight made vision easy, but also exposed him. He had darkened his body with mud first. Still, he stuck to cover as much as possible as he eased into the little pueblo.

He knew sentries would be posted and that he had to locate them. Luckily, the drunken scouts were undisciplined. Before long he had spotted the guards, for each of them carelessly skylighted himself.

Touch the Sky calculated which of the sentries would be easiest to reach from his present position. Before he set out, an image surfaced in his mind, the image of Honey Eater lying on the ground, her lifeblood seeping out around the haft of Big Tree's knife.

Big Tree. Why not make a nervous sweat break out all over that red tyrant?

Softly but clearly, Touch the Sky made the sound of the owl hoot. These debauched *pistoleros*

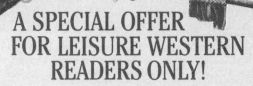

GET FOUR BOOKS TOTALLY *FREE*—A VALUE BETWEEN $16 AND $20

would pay it little attention. But Big Tree would know exactly what it meant.

Again Touch the Sky watched the silhouetted figure atop the house just to his right. Then, after briefly touching the medicine pouch on his clout, the Cheyenne began low-crawling toward the house.

Chapter Eight

"Bless my ass," grumbled Victorio Robles, rolling out of the warm nest of his bedroll.

He had just been kicked awake so that he could begin his stint of guard duty on the roofs. *Maldito,* but it was cold up here in the mountains at night! He shivered as he stepped into his boots and buckled on his leather gunbelt.

Victorio and several other men had confiscated a little house a stone's throw away from the cantina in Santa Rosa. The rightful owners had been forced to move in with relatives across the plaza— Poco Loco was the only "law" in this territory, so whatever his deputies did was legal.

Victorio's head still throbbed from his drunk of the night before. But he took a hair off the dog, lifting a bottle of mescal to his lips and drinking his breakfast. Thus fortified for guard duty, he stumbled out into the grainy predawn darkness.

Santa Rosa was as still and quiet as a graveyard. Thin pockets of mist floated in the streets like silent ghosts, and behind the mountains in the east the first hint of sunrise lightened the sky. A dog howled mournfully at the edge of town, and Victorio could hear his boots scraping in the dirt.

Peaceful enough. All this panic over one Indian who made a lucky shot. Victorio shrugged. *Indios* were pissants. The priests claimed they did not have souls. Without a soul, one could not show courage or great skill as a warrior.

He arrived at an adobe house at the outskirts of the village.

"Roberto," he called to the man up on the roof. "Throw down the ladder."

There was no response.

Victorio raised his voice. "Roberto, you fool! If Poco Loco finds out you fell asleep on guard duty, he will flay your soles. *Eres un necio?* Are you a fool? Now, throw down the ladder!"

Still nothing. The fool wasn't just asleep, Victorio realized. He must also be drunk.

Cursing, Victorio went inside the deserted house and scrounged around until he found an old piece of rope. He went back outside and managed to toss the rope around one of the vigas, the logs that protruded from the top edge of the adobe.

"You son of a worthless whore, Roberto," he muttered as he hauled himself up the wall. Such exertion, with a hangover, made his stomach flutter with nausea.

"You stinking sot!" Victorio pulled himself up

onto the roof. He glanced around until he spotted Roberto, curled up in sleep at the far corner of the roof. "Wake up, you worthless dungheap," Victorio barked, crossing to the sentry and kicking him in the leg.

Nothing. Growling with irritation, Victorio reached down, gripped Roberto's jacket, and tugged him around onto his back.

"*¡Ay Dios!*"

Shock slammed into Victorio like a body blow, and he made the sign of the cross. He leaped backward, his breath snagging in his throat.

Roberto's head lolled back as if connected to his neck by only a string. His throat gaped open in a raw, red, obscene grin of death. The stench of death fouled the air.

Most shocking of all, however, was the gaping hole in Roberto's chest where the Cheyenne had quite literally ripped out his heart.

"But, *jefe*," complained an agitated Esteban, speaking for the rest of the men. "That red bastard tore Roberto's heart from his very chest! *Madre de Dios!* It is still missing. He is a demon from hell, and I say he ate that heart!"

"He did not eat it," Big Tree said quietly—so quietly that the rest gathered around the Tres Hermanas ignored him. They were busy staring at Poco Loco, waiting for his response.

The leader of the pistoleros was unsure how to handle this thing. Here it was, barely after sunrise. He *should* be sound asleep until at least noon. Then he would usually have a woman or a girl brought to his bed for some fun.

Instead, this flea-bitten blanket ass from up north had disrupted his life completely. Poco Loco was starting to feel the warmth of a slow-simmering rage.

"He has killed two of us in two days," Victorio chimed in, his face still drained of color after the discovery of Roberto's corpse. "I am no coward—I fixed bayonets against the gringos at Cerro Gordo! But this now, it is different. Tonight, when the sun goes down, who will be the next to die?"

"And why has he been able to kill again?" Poco Loco asked. "Are you by-God men or a bunch of *perfumados*? He never should have been allowed into town in the first place."

"Must we stop the wind from blowing, too?" Esteban demanded. "This *indio* moves like a shadow."

Poco Loco's deadly scattergun was up in a moment, both muzzles staring at Esteban.

"Is the cow bellowing to the bull?" the *jefe* asked, quiet menace marking his tone.

"Look at both of you," Big Tree scoffed. "Doing exactly what the Cheyenne wants you to do—acting like a bunch of panicked women."

Poco Loco frowned so deeply, his shaggy eyebrows met. "You are the one who brought this curse in among us, Big Tree."

"Yes, and I will kill him. And then you will profit from the kill, for the money is yours. But all of you must show your courage. He is deliberately working at us, driving a wedge between us. If we let him succeed, he will destroy us. But if we get into lockstep and stay there, he is worm fodder."

Poco Loco took heart at these words. "Big Tree

is right. This fight is ours to win. Today we will scour the hills around this town. If he is holed up anywhere near here, we will rout him!"

Esteban and the rest seemed to draw a little comfort from their *jefe*'s confidence.

"Now you're acting like men with stones on them," Poco Loco approved, throwing his fiber morral onto the table. "Good liquor for all! I have a bottle of officer's whiskey, taken from the saddlebags of that *capitán* we killed yesterday."

The men cheered, for everybody knew the best whiskey in Mexico was reserved for the army. Poco Loco pulled a bottle out, then immediately frowned.

The bottle felt greasy. He looked closer and saw that the dark brown glass was covered with blood! Only now did he notice that the sack, too, was stained with wetness. Poco Loco turned it over on the table, and something wet and solid plopped out. He glanced at it in curiosity for only a moment, then felt the gorge rise in his throat when he realized it was Roberto's missing heart!

About midmorning, with their shadows slanting slightly west, Knobby called out, "Here they come!"

Touch the Sky, busy rigging something over the narrow opening of their limestone cave, spoke without turning around.

"Let 'em. We won't bother to cover the sign we were here. I know Big Tree. He'll make sure one of the Mexicans goes in the cave first."

"Just mind your business there," Knobby warned him. "That-ere snake gets loose, you'll git

a heap more 'n just sick. That's a Sonora rattler—
twice the pizen as the American rattler. Saw a
feller up and bit by one near Copper Canyon. That
poor hoss swole up big as a hog 'fore he croaked."

"Shut your damn mouth," Touch the Sky
snapped, nervous sweat oozing at Knobby's vivid
description. Knobby had caught the snake by
crawling out into some sunny rocks just after daylight. It was trapped in a thin piece of hide that
had been quickly folded over on it and stitched
shut with an awl and sinew. Then, working
through the cloth, they clipped off the tiny rattler.
And several chunks of jerked meat had been
shoved into the pouch too, so whoever found it
would think it was a food cache and open it
quickly.

He hid it well enough to look like a cache, but
not so well that it would not be easy to find.

"There," he said, backing out of the cave. "With
a little luck, that's three men down."

"Ahuh," Knobby said, his voice grim. "And with
a little o' the wrong luck, we'll be looking up at
daisies! They're formin' into three search parties
right now. Big Tree and two Mexicans leading
'em."

"No more cold camps up here," Touch the Sky
decided as he gathered up his kit and rigging.
"We'll get the horses and keep them with us from
here on out."

Knobby watched him shrewdly. Below, some of
the men were already fanning into the foothills.

"I see which way the wind sets," Knobby finally
said. "You wouldn't be keeping the horses 'lessen

you expected a running battle. You mean to drive them out of Santa Rosa?"

Touch the Sky nodded. "We can pick away at them, but you see how it is. With them forted up, we'll run out of camps around here. Put them on the run, they're bound to slip up."

The old trapper looked a little doubtful, but he nodded nonetheless. "Every major battle in history was won with either a quick slaughter or a running fight. I 'spect thissen won't be no different."

"No," Touch the Sky said quietly, jacking a round into the chamber of his rifle and watching the searchers move up from the valley. "No different at all."

"God-*damn* that whoreson Indian!" Poco Loco fumed, watching his man Benito writhe in the dirt like a man in a seizure.

"The poison is working on his brain already," Big Tree said casually, sliding his big .44 from the holster and thumbing it back to full cock. Esteban started to object, but Big Tree coolly blew a hole through Benito's pomaded head.

The snake had escaped into the cave when the men leaped back from the entrance.

"I noticed," Poco Loco said, his eyes slanting toward Big Tree, "how you fell back and let Benito go in first."

Big Tree grinned. "I'll send a priest to console his widow. Nor did I see you rush forward to save your man."

Poco Loco, despite his surly mood, could not help grinning at Big Tree's brutal honesty. This was a man who gave it to you raw and real, with the bark still on it. That is why, despite their mutual animosity and distrust, they had always admired each other.

But the men . . . they had never tangled with Indians from the north country, proud Indians who perhaps knew too much of warfare.

"Big Tree," he said quietly while some of the others dug a grave for Benito. "We may have to flee this place. I have another stronghold. It is in a better position. I am for staying right here. But the men—once it reaches a certain point, they must either be given something to do or they will rebel. You know that?"

The Comanche thought about this. "And if we are in motion, he too must be in motion. That exposes us, but he must take more chances too."

"*Preciso*. However, this place—it is a hard climb to reach it. I will wait one more night here in Santa Rosa and see if our noble red man strikes again."

Chapter Nine

"The place is called San Sebastian," Poco Loco explained as he banged open the door of an iron stove and stirred the embers to life with an old broom handle. "I holed up there once during the war. So remote the place has never been sacked."

"Remote won't matter," Big Tree objected. "If an eagle can get to it, so can Touch the Sky."

"He can get to it, of course. But he will have to show himself to do it. He will have to cross a vast *jornada*, then climb through barren pinnacles. Unlike this place, which sets low and offers cover all around, San Sebastian is atop a long, barren spine of mountains."

Poco Loco lifted the lid from a blue-enameled coffeepot and tossed in a piece of eggshell to boil with the beans. He set it on the flat iron top of the stove. Both men had holed up in the reinforced cantina with a sentry outside all night long.

"San Sebastain was made from heavy stone," Poco Loco said. "Those buildings will be there when God retires."

"And the residents? They will not fight?"

Poco Loco, busy breaking open his scattergun to check the loads, looked at the Comanche and smiled. "There is the beauty of it, compadre. There are no residents. The people who lived there were inordinately fond of dogs. Kept hundreds of them around. Then rabies swept through the region, and the people were either killed or driven off. The place is so remote, no one has settled there again."

Big Tree considered all this as he huddled under his sleeping robe, waiting for the stove's warmth to penetrate the chill. "It might do," he finally agreed. "But it would be better if we could kill the Cheyenne right here."

"If pigs had wings, they could fly, amigo." Poco Loco snapped closed the breech of his gun and dropped it into its special sling over his hip. "I told you yesterday, I do not look forward to this flight. I would rather kill him here, too. But you see how it is with the men. They will rebel if I simply force them to sit here in this hollow while we are picked off like beef cattle."

A sudden scuffing of gravel outside made Big Tree swing up from his robes, big-framed .44 in his fist.

Poco Loco laughed. "Lower your hammer, Quohada! It is only Esteban. He is calling out the men for roll call. I want to be sure our sneaky friend did not come calling in the night."

Poco Loco poured coffee into a pottery mug.

"Three men he has killed so far, Big Tree. You are right that a run to San Sebastian will expose us. But we are clearly vulnerable anyway, yet the Cheyenne is not. The effort will be worth it if his head is truly worth so much gold."

Outside, Esteban called out, "Lupe!"

"Yo!"

"Ernesto!"

"Present!"

"You know," Big Tree said quietly, "the Cheyenne is not alone? There is one other man with him."

Poco Loco stopped his cup halfway to his lips and stared at the other man. "Amigo, you are like the whores in Mexico City, you know that? You name one price when you show your tits, another when you remove your skirts. You did not tell me all this at once, for you knew I would tell you to pull stakes and keep riding. So, what about this second man?"

"I know only that he wears leather boots and his feet slew outward when he walks, like a hair-face, not an Indian. I found prints they did not bother to hide."

As he heard the men answer to roll call outside, Poco Loco's somber face began to relax. "Well, we will take what good news we can. At least it sounds like the men are all accounted for—he did not strike in the night. Perhaps we will not have to flee this place after all."

Outside, Esteban shouted, "Manuel?"

Dead silence.

"Manuel? Manuel Torres?"

Silence, as thick and deep as the folds around a

country graveyard. Poco Loco and Big Tree exchanged a long glance.

"Is Manuel a heavy sleeper?" Big Tree asked.

Poco Loco frowned. "The man is always up with the birds."

Big Tree nodded, seeing how things stood. "He will not be getting up this morning," he said quietly. "And we will be riding for San Sebastian."

Touch the Sky and Knobby did not risk another camp after the discovery of their previous one. Instead, they simply stayed in motion, keeping their horses immediately to hand and taking turns sleeping in two-hour shifts while one of them stayed on guard. This way the horses continued to graze fresh grass and get plenty of rest for the ordeal both men knew was coming.

"They know about victim number four by now," Knobby said. "That'll tear it, you watch. You'll get your wish. They'll be pulling foot today."

Touch the Sky nodded. The two of them sat behind the cover of a sandstone shoulder well above Santa Rosa. They could see, in the gathering sunlight, men milling about in the plaza below.

"They'll ride," he agreed. "Big Tree won't just sit and wait. He's smart enough to know he has to use natural advantages. They'll ride to some spot where we can't use ground cover and high ground against them."

"Ain't just Big Tree," Knobby said. "We got to worry about the pepper-gut, too, the one called Poco Loco. You saw them Injuns' eyes when they said his name. I got a good look at his ugly, scarred pan yestiddy. 'At sumbich is crazy as dogs in the hot moon."

Knobby lapsed into a moody silence for a spell, gnawing on a cold biscuit he'd been saving in his possibles bag. Both men looked rough. The need to stay in motion kept them exhausted, yet old Knobby steadfastly refused to do less than a man's share. If Touch the Sky tried to let him sleep more than two hours, the old man would come awake on his own, grumbling about ignorant savages who couldn't keep white man's time. Like all mountain men, he believed a man had to pull his own freight so long as he walked the earth.

"Sprout," he said now, cautiously. "You 'member a saying your pa likes? One about the pitcher and the well?"

Touch the Sky thought for a minute, running through a list of John Hanchon's favorite sayings. Then he grinned. "Sure. 'The pitcher can go once too often to the well.' "

Knobby nodded. "That's the one. I just wunner— you think maybe you're doin' that now? I mean, by killin' off them Mexers one by one before you do for Big Tree? Ain't the point to kill him, not these others?"

Touch the Sky said nothing, mulling the old man's words. After all, the point *was* to rid the world of Big Tree. He was letting his rage over Honey Eater's ordeal color his motives. But what if he did go once too often to the well? What if he was killed hacking at a branch, while the root— Big Tree—escaped damage?

"A warrior," Knobby added, "is 'sposed to stay

frosty and shoot plumb. You kill from the head, not the gut."

Finally, Touch the Sky nodded. "You're right, old-timer. Revenge shouldn't even enter the mix. Never mind tormenting Big Tree. Let's kill that red son of the Wendigo and get the hell out of here."

But even Knobby, who had spent plenty of time south of the Rio Grande, had forgotten what the country to the west of them was like. Touch the Sky's new resolve to kill Big Tree without delay was rendered meaningless by the more immediate problem of staying alive themselves.

The Jornada del Muerto, or Desert of Death, stretched for an unrelenting eighty miles. Old Knobby had wisely made crude sunshades for men and horses, fashioning them out of rawhide flaps with eye slits in them. These proved indispensable, for the white alkali sand and broad gypsum flats reflected an unrelenting glare, one that could drive men and beasts mad if unprotected.

The terrain was hard on the horses. Loose sand taxed their ankles and drifted over sharp-edged rocks and shale that could trip them up and cut them. Water was scarce, and only the survival skills of a hard life spent on the frontier saved the two friends. Old streambeds that seemed bone dry could yield a little water if you dug into them a few feet; the hollow tops of boulders that never saw sunlight often held pools of rainwater.

There was also the problem of visibility.

Finding sign was no problem, for their enemies were not trying to hide their movements. The pursuers had kept a respectful distance, following the boiling cloud of dust. But as they had feared, snipers were left behind in wallows to rise up and shoot at them. One bullet had sliced through Touch the Sky's rigging, spooking his coyote dun. About an hour later, a surprise sniper killed one of the ponies on Knobby's string.

"That does it," Touch the Sky announced. His lips were set in the tight line that foretold an enemy's death. "Time to play a trick I learned from Big Tree himself."

Working quickly, Touch the Sky and Knobby gathered enough wiry palomilla grass to stuff a crude buckskin suit. They put the fake rider up on the dun and tied it down.

"Just keep riding west," Touch the Sky directed, cutting a fast little roan off his string. He swung up onto its back and laid his Sharps across the withers. "I'll be back."

First he rode due east, backtracking. Then he cut north, pushing the spirited mustang to a powerful gallop. When he guessed he might be somewhere behind the next sniper's position, Touch the Sky reined in his pony and hobbled it behind a craggy mound of rocks.

He did not bother with concealed movement. Others out ahead might spot him, so he concentrated only on speed as his eyes desperately swept the deep browns and parched yellows of the arid terrain.

There! He had just spotted a glint of reflection off to his left. A moment later he grinned, thanking the Mexican male's love of hammered silver: A man was hunkered in a wallow, drawing a bead on the distant figures approaching. It was the silver conchos on his sombrero that gave him away.

Touch the Sky had no idea if the sniper was dropping a bead on the dummy rider or Old Knobby. The Cheyenne didn't waste a moment. First, he unleashed a shrill war cry to interrupt the Mexican's shot.

The man whirled, bringing the muzzle of a carbine with him. Touch the Sky squeezed his trigger, then heard the most sickening sound in the world, bad powder fizzling in his primer load!

The Mexican's carbine barked at the same moment Touch the Sky twisted in midair, minimizing the target. The bullet burned across his chest like a white-hot wire of pain, opening a thin line of blood. The Mexican jacked in another round even as Touch the Sky leaped, swinging his rifle like a war club.

The solid wood stock caught him on the point of the jaw, rocking his head back hard and knocking his sombrero off. Touch the Sky wrenched the carbine from him, tapped the muzzle into his chest, and fired point blank. The Mexican's heels were still scratching the dirt as the Cheyenne raced back toward Knobby.

"That's five down," Knobby greeted him with a poker face. "But I'm guessing it wasn't Big Tree you done for?"

Touch the Sky shook his head, gazing ahead toward that roiling cloud of dust on the horizon.

"No," he answered. "I can make all the vows I want to. But Big Tree has his own plans, and mainly he plans to be the last one to die."

Chapter Ten

Meantime, far to the north in the Powder River country, Medicine Flute's treacherous plan was being carried out.

Crow Killer, leader of the Bullwhip soldier society, picked two good riders. One was sent far south to the red-rock country, the other about half that distance. Both were to send up false smoke messages—one intended to travel south for Touch the Sky, the other north for the Cheyenne camp.

Naturally, the lie was received up north first, for that rider had less distance to travel. Soon after the camp crier raced through the paths, shouting the news of Touch the Sky's death, his worst tribal enemies had gathered at Medicine Flute's tipi.

"Did you hear, brothers?" gloated a triumphant Wolf Who Hunts Smiling. "Did you hear it? When his she-bitch Honey Eater heard of it, the women of her clan were forced to surround her. Even now they are watching her. Only the constant reminder of her child has restrained her from falling on a knife."

"Even better," added Crow Killer, "is watching the stunned look on the faces of Little Horse, Two Twists, and Tangle Hair. His men look like drunks who have woken up in the wrong country! Even now they are huddled in Little Horse's tipi, crying in each other's arms."

"They are not crying," Wolf Who Hunts Smiling corrected him. "Not those three. They are laying plans. But let them. We are safe. Without their think-piece, Touch the Sky, they are helpless. Too, we are far away from the supposed crime, and they have no cause to draw blood in camp."

"It would be worth a little blood," Medicine Flute said. "The pleasure of seeing their faces, of hearing his whore cry out to the holy ones, has been worth it. I only hope our little trick turns out to be no fooling. That is up to Big Tree."

Wolf Who Hunts Smiling nodded. "Only one pleasure could be greater, and we must miss seeing it. I mean when White Man Runs Him reads sign that his woman is supposedly dead. Bucks, he will make a groan from his soul that could make a dead man weep with pity."

"I tell you, 'manos," said the pistolero named Ernesto. "It was I who found Luis. I tell you this—whatever struck his jaw hit with such force it snapped the head back hard enough to break his neck!"

"This indio," Ricardo said, "cannot be a mere

mortal. Has anyone seen him? Five times he has come among us and killed, yet who has seen him?"

"Yes," said Juan. "He is invisible and he has supernatural strength—the strength of ten men! This Big Tree, he has brought a northern devil in among us!"

Five of the remaining *pistoleros* had gathered in a little circle during a brief rest. Earlier, a sandstorm from Mexico's interior plateau had pelted them in a yellow wall of fury. Now a hot sphere of merciless sun blazed overhead, relentlessly driving the temperature up into triple digits. Sweat poured through the grime on their faces, making little mud streaks.

Esteban had been passing close enough to hear the last remarks. *"Vaya!"* he exclaimed. "Don't be fools. Would a supernatural devil have to use Luis's own weapon against him? This Cheyenne, he is a good killer, yes. But he was born of woman, hombres, and he can die like any man."

"Perhaps," Ricardo responded. "But he can kill better than most."

Esteban shook his head like a man who had seen the big animal. He nodded across the barren flat to the place where Big Tree and Poco Loco were hunkered in parley.

"So can Big Tree," Esteban said. "I was with him and Poco Loco when that Comanche shot out the eye of a Texas Ranger with an arrow at five hundred yards. The left eye—he did it on a bet."

"That was a Texas Ranger," Juan said. "No men to fool with, yet men you can *see*. How do you shoot the eye out of a man who never shows himself?"

Desert Manhunt

Esteban turned to stare into the windswept wasteland behind them. "He will show himself," he predicted confidently. "And when he does, the readiness is all."

"He won't get another one of us," Poco Loco swore with grim determination as he mopped sweat from his face with a limp, filthy bandanna.

He pointed due west. "See those two pinnacles rising side by side? San Sebastian lies between them. We will be there by nightfall if we encounter no more sandstorms."

"It is not sandstorms that worry me," Big Tree replied, casting a sideways glance toward the little knot of men. "Are you sure of your men?"

Poco Loco scowled. "Esteban is a good man, he will keep them bunched. But I do not blame them for scheming. You rode in among us singing songs of easy gold. Now, five dead comrades later, we see the gold is not so easy."

"Your 'comrades,'" Big Tree said sarcastically, "are shiftless, down-at-the-heels criminals who would shoot their own mothers for a plugged peso. You don't think about the dead ones any more than you think about the beans you ate yesterday."

Despite his weariness, the leader of the Mexican gang laughed outright, flashing strong white teeth.

"You know me well, amigo," he said. "If I can't eat it, drink it, or rut on it, I throw it away! No, I don't care about the men, Big Tree. But I need their firepower. How can we hold off *federales* and other gangs without firepower?"

"Granted," Big Tree said. Then he grinned slyly and added, "But three thousand in gold, especially in this poor nation where men labor for thirty cents a day, is a tidy sum, is it not? That would help a man recruit new followers."

Poco Loco nodded, catching the renegade's drift. Either way, Big Tree was arguing, Poco Loco came out of this ahead—assuming, of course, that the Cheyenne finally tripped up and got himself killed. That reward money could either outfit this gang or recruit a new one.

"He will kill no more of us," Poco Loco said again, gauging the distance to those twin pinnacles. He rose with a grunt of protest and slapped his hat on his thigh to dislodge the dust.

"Vamanos!" he shouted across to the rest of the men. "Let's go, boys! And from here on out, keep your thoughts bloody!"

"I figured out where they're aimin' to," Knobby said, his voice rasping harshly from a throatful of dirt. He pointed toward two distant pinnacles of rock on the western horizon. "That's the Sangre de Cristo range. Blood of Christ mountains. I ain't never seed it, but talk has it there's a lost pueblo up there. A whole village what's been deserted. They're goin' for the high ground."

Touch the Sky said nothing, but his friend's words made sense. Too damn much sense, he thought. The idea of attacking high ground would worry an experienced warrior at any time. But especially now, when Touch the Sky and Knobby were already balanced on the verge of exhaustion.

It wasn't just the daunting odds. Their enemy

were able to sleep, take regular meals, relax their guard now and then by posting sentries. Touch the Sky and Knobby, in harsh contrast, had to face a grim reality—they simply couldn't keep this grueling contest up much longer. Grain for the ponies was dangerously low, and graze was virtually nonexistent out here on the *jornada*.

Yes, he had managed to kill five men. But look how many remained. More important, look *who* remained. Big Tree. And now, with his reserves of strength almost tapped out, Touch the Sky had to face the hardest phase of the battle.

Needs must when the devil drives. That was another favorite saying of John Hanchon. And Touch the Sky knew his white father was right. One way or another, it had to get done. Big Tree had left Honey Eater for dead, and for that he must die.

"Well," Knobby said, cutting into the Cheyenne's thoughts, "they're ridin' again, see their puffs? One thing for sure, they ain't sendin' any more snipers back. Looks like we won't be able to take out any more of 'em on the trail."

Touch the Sky started to reply. But at that moment something caught his eye—smoke sign, rising up from the headlands north of the Rio Grande. Kiowa Apache country, he guessed.

He watched the columns and puffs rise in a careful sequence, various shapes symbolizing specific tribes and warriors. His nape began to tingle when he saw that it was word from his own tribe.

Knobby, too, spotted the smoke. "What's the word, sprout?" he demanded in a dusty croak. "My sign's a little rusty."

"News from Powder River," the warrior replied tersely, his eyes squinting. Sweat broke out on his face when he saw the "cut-off cloud," an abruptly truncated smoke signal that symbolized a death.

"What news?" Knobby persisted.

Touch the Sky held silent, forgetting to take his next breath as he watched the long, thin column rise. The symbol for a woman.

"Well, what damn news?" Knobby demanded.

Touch the Sky's face drained cold as death when he read the last symbol—three quick puffs that symbolized the tribe's shaman.

Touch the Sky had no idea how long he sat there, his shocked mind simply shutting down in the face of this brutal news. When he finally came to awareness again, Knobby was gently shaking him. The old man's face was white as moonstone.

"Katy Christ, Matthew," he said softly. "You look like you just got a peek into hell itself. What is it, boy?"

"Honey Eater," Touch the Sky managed, the words coming up out of his throat like nails tearing at it. "She is dead."

Big Tree had no way of knowing about the newest conspiracy up north—the plan to make Touch the Sky believe his woman had died. So he felt his pulse thudding with dread when he, too, spotted that smoke sign north of the border.

So he had killed Touch the Sky's woman, after all? Big Tree felt the forbidden thrill of a child who has stolen a valuable object. Yes, it was his, and it was a thrill to have it. But surely he must pay for the crime.

Pay? If Touch the Sky saw that sign, the very Wendigo himself was about to be unleashed.

The Comanche let his cayuse slow until Poco Loco caught up with him.

"Amigo," Big Tree said, "tell the men to move their weapons to full cock. Trouble is coming, and soon."

Poco Loco laughed. "*Vaya!* Look, this is the worst time to attack. The worst place."

The Mexican pointed at the ground, littered with loose lava rock and chunks of half-buried basalt, left centuries earlier by glacial action. It made riding treacherous.

"A horse can barely trot here, much less gallop," Poco Loco pointed out. "And look, no cover at all. We would have a clear shot at him from any direction."

"He is coming," Big Tree insisted, though he did not have the courage to add, he is coming for *me* because I snuffed out the very reason for his existence. The Comanche only hoped one thing, that the Cheyenne would have so much blood in his eyes, he could not see clearly the right course of action. Anger could block a man from his best movements. And a split second's mistake was all Big Tree required.

"Good, let him come," Poco Loco said confidently. "I have been wanting a look at this big Indian."

All too soon, however, Poco Loco got his wish.

Big Tree had noticed the dust spirals approaching from their right flank long before any of the others. It was Esteban who first raised a warning.

"Rider approaching!"

Poco Loco broke out his field glasses, then handed them to Big Tree. "Is this our man, Quohada?"

Big Tree took one swift look and nodded. "The very man."

"What is he doing?" Poco Loco asked. "Is he a fool? Surely he means to stop well out from us and take a shot?"

But soon it was clear that the Cheyenne approaching them had no interest in sniping from afar. His rifle, muzzle thrust toward the sky, rested butt-first on his thigh. His left hand clutched his red-streamered war lance. He used no hands to ride, merely clinging with his knees.

"Here comes my gold!" Poco Loco sang out as he leaped down from his horse and started shouting orders. "Esteban! Quickly! Have the men scoop out wallows. Jorges! You and Ricardo lead the horses farther back out of range. The rest, check your loads! More than one of us is going to air him out! Let's see who scores the fatal hit!"

Big Tree, however, looked far less sanguine. This magnificent warrior wasn't riding in, facing almost certain death, just to shoot at the first pop-up target. He had a purpose in coming.

Big Tree wasted no time. A wallow wouldn't be good enough. Giving it no thought, he shot one of his remuda and forted up behind the dead horse. The Comanche grabbed a handful of arrows and notched the first one on his bowstring, waiting.

Now the drumming hoofbeats could be heard. When Big Tree could see the determined set of Touch the Sky's face, he launched his first arrow. It streaked past just to the left of the approaching

Cheyenne, and that shot sent him into defensive action.

Touch the Sky slid forward and down, gripping the dun's neck. At the same time, his mount began running a zigzagging pattern. Big Tree unleashed more arrows as the first riflemen opened up. Geysers of dirt shot up all around the pony's pounding hooves, and arrows ripped past Touch the Sky so swiftly and close that the fletching burned his skin.

"The fool!" Poco Loco screamed. "If he keeps coming, he will be in range of my shotgun! Hit him, you blind fools!"

A bullet passed through Touch the Sky's rawhide shirt, tugging at it. Another ripped through his buffalo-hair halter. But now he could see the place where Big Tree was hunkered down, launching arrows from behind that dead horse.

"Jesus, Joseph, and Mary, *hit* him!" Poco Loco screamed. Ricardo leaped up from his wallow, drawing a clear shot on the Cheyenne. Touch the Sky's rifle bucked, and a red smear replaced the Mexican's face. Big Tree stopped firing arrows, tensing his muscles for what was coming. He would have to be quick to avoid a hard death.

Jorges turned to leap out of the Indian's path, and a moment later the war lance punched through his chest from behind. And now the lethal maniac on that magnificent horse was bearing down on Big Tree, his obsidian eyes livid with hatred. One hand went to the knife in his belt even as he prepared to leap.

Big Tree sprang hard to the right just as Poco Loco's scattergun roared with a deafening explosion. Touch the Sky, on the verge of leaping, missed the main brunt of the buckshot. But a smattering of pellets slammed into his chest, tearing away skin and knocking him backward so that he almost fell off his horse.

The dun, too, took some of the pellets, staggering hard. But the well-trained mount doggedly charged on, clearing the group of men and heading off into the vastness behind them.

Touch the Sky managed to turn around once and meet Big Tree's frightened eyes. "You are dead, Quohada!" the Cheyenne yelled. "From where you stand now to the place where the sun goes down, there is no safe place for you! If you go into breastworks, I will drive you out! I swear it by the four directions, and the Holy Ones hear me. Before I ride north again, you will be dead!"

Chapter Eleven

Knobby definitely did not like his companion's grim, trancelike silence. They rode on in no particular hurry now, for Big Tree and the panicked Mexicans had broken for the slope after Touch the Sky's bold assault. But the Cheyenne, Knobby told himself, now appeared like a dead man with his eyes open.

At one point, Knobby saw Matthew's leg brush hard against a sharp-spined prickly pear, ripping deep gashes—yet the warrior never even glanced down! It might as well have been a gnat landing on him, for all that he even knew of it.

A dead man with his eyes open . . . that's what Matthew was, all right, Knobby thought. He was too exhausted to complete this mission in high country. I'm the one with snow in the eaves,

Knobby told himself. But that young buck has done all the fighting.

"That was a nice piece o' horsemanship back there," Knobby said quietly. "You trimmed 'em by two more, sprout. That leaves only five Mexers, countin' the *jefe* and that shotgun of his. But it also leaves Big Tree."

Knobby waited. Their tired mounts stopped now and then to blow as they began the ascent into the mountains. Leather creaked, Knobby's bit ring chinked, but no sound from the Cheyenne. The old man wasn't even sure he'd heard him just now.

"We got Big Tree left," Knobby repeated, "and you goin' at him in the high country. It don't bode good, boy! I say you need rest. They ain't goin' nowhere in a hurry, you—"

"Whack the cork, old-timer," Touch the Sky cut him off. "I don't need rest. All I need is the hair of the mother-rutting son of a bitch who killed my wife."

Knobby scowled. "So to hell with common sense, huh? Well, looks like Big Tree has kilt your boy's ma—you gonna cost him his pa, too, with your bullheaded, cussed stubbornness? Don't take no Philadelphia lawyer to prove that we're both beat out."

Those words sank through somewhat, and Touch the Sky gave his friend a long look.

"What do you mean, 'looks like' Big Tree killed my wife?"

"Looks like," Knobby snapped. "That's what I said. What, did I switch to Chinee on you, boy?

Hell, you saw some smoke up in the clouds. Is that truth writ in blood?"

Knobby said no more. But the words he had just spoken fell on Touch the Sky's ears like rain to dry earth. Knobby wasn't saying the word about Honey Eater was not true—but he was saying it *could* be a lie. For a moment, hope surged inside Touch the Sky like a swelling bubble. But he refused to let himself grasp at this possibility—for then, the discovery that his woman was indeed in the Land of Ghosts would hit doubly hard. Finally Touch the Sky said:

"Straight words, Knobby. We'll make a cold camp when we hit the slope."

"Now you're talkin' like John Hanchon's boy. We need sleep, chuck in our bellies. This hoss'll tell you somethin' else, too."

Knobby used his left elbow to tap the walnut stock of the Kentucky rifle in his saddle boot. "So far I've let you take care of the killin' because this was your battle. I come along to be your guide. But you can't do it alone from here on out—not up there in them peaks. Either both of us bust caps, tadpole, or both of us will be lookin' up to see grass."

Touch the Sky raised his eyes to look at those two gray pinnacles prodding into the blue belly of the sky. Old Knobby had already done his job— but the old trapper was right. This was no time, the warrior cautioned himself, to let grief sway his decisions. He must put the grief away from his mind. His enemies would like nothing better than to see him swollen with rage, berserk, and thus incapable of the cool decisions that often determine a battle.

"It's me and you, old campaigner," Touch the Sky finally said. "And I don't care how long in the tooth you are—a man couldn't ask for a better partner when his bacon is in the fire."

Touch the Sky's insane but effective charge had left Poco Loco's surviving men in the grip of panic. No one bothered to bury Ricardo or Jorges—indeed, no one even broke out a rosary and prayed over them. It had become every man for himself, and the devil take the hindmost. And the name of this devil was Touch the Sky.

"Big Tree," Poco Loco fumed when the two men could not be overheard, "I saw that savage's face! Man, I never saw the kill light in a man's eyes like that. He was possessed by a demon. Whatever you did to him, it was a mistake. I know this kind— hurt one of his, he kills two of yours."

Even as he spoke, Poco Loco craned around in the saddle to stare down the narrow, rocky trail behind them. Esteban, still loyal despite his abject fear, had wisely taken up the drag position—that way none of the four *pistoleros* could bolt back down the mountain.

Not that a wise man would, Poco Loco thought—not with that red killing machine trailing them. But men were seldom wise once their nerves frazzled like worn ropes.

Big Tree, unlike the Mexicans, showed nothing in his face. It remained an inscrutable stone mask. But he, too, had seen the preternatural hatred and need for vengeance in Touch the Sky's eyes. Yes, the Cheyenne had let Sis-ki-dee go, up in Bloody Bones Canyon, when the Blackfoot begged for mercy. But even begging for mercy—a humiliation Indians considered worse than outright defeat—was out of the question for the man who killed Honey Eater.

Therefore, Big Tree saw clearly how things stood. He must kill Touch the Sky before Touch the Sky killed him. And since there was no distance he could run to escape the Cheyenne, what better place than this sierra—and what better time than now?

A sudden snarl of rage abruptly interrupted Big Tree's thoughts. For a heartbeat, he thought one of the nervous men had finally gone mad with fear—or worse, that Touch the Sky had got the jump on him.

Then he saw it: the brindled fur of a dog watching them from a ledge of rock just overhead. A wild dog, at least half wolf, Big Tree thought—and a steady stream of saliva rolled off its lolling tongue, a sure sign of rabies. He had heard of it happening before: A virulent strain of rabies could haunt an area, infecting generations of dogs.

In one smooth, steady motion, he pulled the .44 from its holster and snapped off a round. It caught the dog in the chest and flipped him back off the ledge.

"There'll be more than one around here," Big Tree said. "Keep a red eye out."

"Best be careful when we reach San Sebastian," Poco Loco said. "We may have to clear the buildings of dogs."

Big Tree nodded. But looking up toward the

ledge, after he killed the dog, had given him an idea.

"This is the only way up?" he demanded of Poco Loco. "You are sure of it?"

"Does asparagus make your piss stink? Of course I am sure of it. The back of the range is all cliffs."

"Good." Big Tree grinned, his old fighting spirit returning. Was he not a Quohada Comanche, one of the feared Red Raiders of the Plains? Which tribe had cleared Texas and driven almost every white-eyed bastard from the Arizona Territory? Indeed, which tribe, according to the white man's newspapers, had killed more hair-face settlers than any other?

Big Tree said, "Our noble red man is distraught with grief. He will not be focused as a warrior must be. Why should his ride up the slope be uneventful?"

Poco Loco was too tired and snappish for girls' guessing games. "If you drift near a point, compadre, make it."

"Just keep riding," Big Tree said. "I'm going up to that ledge. I'll catch up with you later."

When they were well up the slope, the crude trail narrowed and forced Touch the Sky and Knobby to ride single file. The Cheyenne took the point position.

They had tethered their remounts at the bottom of the slope near a little runoff rill that provided some water and scant grass. Both men knew it would not be a horse battle up topside, but close-in fighting. Unlike their enemy, however, they had no exact idea of what lay above, the layout of the place, what natural cover it provided.

Both men were also veterans of frontier violence, and knew better than to expect an easy ride up. They kept their weapons at the ready as they ascended, scanning every nook and cranny for hidden marksmen.

Now more than ever Touch the Sky applied the skills of the warrior, skills taught in training and honed in the hard school of experience. He watched from his side vision as much as from his forward vision. Constantly he slid to the ground to place his fingertips against the sensitive rock, reading it for motion vibrations.

Nor did he ignore the coyote dun's sensitive nostrils. Cheyennes taught their horses to hate the smell of enemy tribes.

Even now, through his red waves of exhaustion, Touch the Sky was aware of it: that tiny prickling in the nape of his neck, the shaman's "third eye" warning him of danger. He turned around and met Knobby's eyes.

The old mountain man nodded. He, too, felt it coming—felt it deep in his old, aching bones. Touch the Sky watched Knobby's thumb reach up and pull the over-and-under's twin hammers back to full cock.

"Easy," Touch the Sky said soothingly into the dun's ear.

Slowly, inexorably, the two men followed the steep, tortuous trail as it wound steadily upward, taking them closer and closer to their meeting with the Black Warrior called Death.

* * *

Big Tree had worked quickly as the rest of his companions continued their ascent toward the deserted pueblo above.

It took coaxing, but his sure-footed cayuse finally climbed over to the ledge beside the trail. As Big Tree had hoped, the opening behind the ledge, into which the dead dog had tumbled, was big enough to conceal his horse.

At one edge of the ledge balanced a massive boulder, perhaps the size of a small pony. Big Tree knew he could not possibly move it by himself, not even with his impressive strength—not on level ground. But the ledge under the boulder was dirt.

Working quickly, keeping a constant eye on the trail below, Big Tree used his knife and his hands to scoop out a little trough in front of the huge boulder. The ledge was not quite level—it tilted a little forward. That angle, plus the rock's formidable weight, should send it plunging straight down if a strong man got his back behind it.

There was just enough space behind it for the Comanche to wedge himself in. He braced his muscle-corded back against the boulder, then slapped both hands against the stone face of the mountain.

Big Tree gave it one little test push, straining hard. He felt the satisfying sensation of the boulder yielding behind him. Grinning, the Comanche relaxed again, letting it return to its normal resting place.

Now it was a question of vigilance and careful timing. Big Tree settled in for the wait, his cold-as-flint eyes watching the trail with unwavering attention.

* * *

Touch the Sky was slowly coaxing the dun around a dogleg bend in the trail when he saw his pony's nostrils suddenly quiver—quivers that led to a snort as the dun recognized the enemy smell.

Touch the Sky's mistake, however, was to first glance right—after all, that was the direction of the sun, and Big Tree always attacked from out of the sun.

That brief mistake made him miss the first shuddering movements of that huge boulder just above them and to their left. By the time Touch the Sky heard Knobby's warning cry, it was too late. His head snapped left just in time to see a huge gray mass blocking out the sky as it plunged downward.

Knobby, right behind his friend, had spotted the rock's motion a split second before Matthew did. He reflexively raised his Kentucky long rifle and swung the muzzle hard, catching the Cheyenne in his left ribs and sweeping him hard off his pony.

But Knobby didn't think he moved in time. And then his own horse was rearing in panic as a resounding crash just ahead of them made it seem like the entire mountain was coming down on them.

Chapter Twelve

"Look at them," Two Twists said, scorn heavy in his voice as he nodded toward the Bullwhips. "That is the second bladder of corn beer they have broached this day. You would think the death of he who may not be named is the Spring Festival to them."

By custom, Two Twists had avoided using Touch the Sky's name, especially since there was a very good chance that he had died an unclean death—killed before he could sing his death song.

Little Horse suddenly threw down the elk steak he had been trying to eat. It landed in the cooking fire outside his tipi and threw sparks on Two Twists and Tangle Hair. Both men flinched, watching him.

"His name is Touch the Sky," Little Horse said

boldly. "What proof do we have that he has gone under?"

The other two gaped. The great flywheel of habit had kept them from questioning smoke sign—especially sign that rose in the Sweetwater Creek region, home of their Sioux allies. But Little Horse was right. Their enemies had shown no respect for anything else. Why not corrupt the moccasin telegraph, too?

"I do not think he is dead," Little Horse added. "And neither does *she*."

All three looked at the lone tipi that sat separately from the others. Honey Eater had insisted on moving back into it. And Little Horse was right. After recovering from her initial grief, Honey Eater had drawn from her deep well of inner strength. She had said nothing about her new resolve to anyone. But Little Horse could see it—she would not believe in the death of Touch the Sky until she had incontrovertible proof.

"You are no shaman," Tangle Hair said slowly, "but you speak straight arrow. How many times have they lied about Touch the Sky? We were fooled because it came in smoke this time. He may indeed be dead. But I agree with you, buck. He is alive until *proven* dead."

Now Two Twists nodded, his young face easing into a grin. "Both of you are so ugly, you shame your mothers. But you are right this time. It is the same with Arrow Keeper. When he disappeared, most ceased to speak his name. But Touch the Sky convinced us we could still name him, for none had seen him die. And truly, has Arrow Keeper left this world? How many times has he warned

Touch the Sky of trouble since his supposed death?"

While Two Twists spoke this last, a group of merrymakers had broken away from the big knot of braves gathered near the Bullwhip lodge.

"Here comes a trouble cloud blowing our way," Tangle Hair said, nodding as the Bullwhips approached them. "Look to your weapons."

"Never mind weapons," Little Horse said. "They are unarmed and led by Medicine Flute. Anything he leads will not involve weapons, only mouth."

The group halted well back from the firepit: Medicine Flute, Wolf Who Hunts Smiling, Crow Killer, Swift Canoe, and several others.

"Bucks," Medicine Flute called out, his voice drunken from long hours of imbibing corn beer, "we wish to console you on the loss of your noble leader, Scrape the Clouds."

This deliberate distortion of Touch the Sky's name drew gales of laughter from the rest. Swift Canoe, stupid as dead wood, did not get the pun at first. When he finally did, he laughed so hard he fell upon the ground in convulsions.

"No, shaman," Crow Killer corrected Medicine Flute, deliberately using Touch the Sky's title to rub it in. "His name was Hit the Heavens!"

More laughter.

"At any rate," Medicine Flute went on, "his name now is In the Ground. And such a tasty bit of a squaw going to waste! Perhaps—"

Medicine Flute never finished his gibe. Indeed, it was some time after that night before he could talk coherently again. Little Horse, who had a deadly throwing aim, always kept a few good-size rocks in his parfleche—when a man was out of bullets in a frenzied fight, they could mean the margin of victory.

Little Horse drew one out, rose up onto his knees, and used his free left hand to aim along as he fired a rock hard at Medicine Flute. It whopped into his mouth with audible force, smashing several teeth, ripping lips and cheeks as they tore into teeth. The force of it knocked Medicine Flute to the ground and evoked a womanish shriek of pain.

"The next two-legged worm among you," Little Horse announced hotly, "who speaks of Touch the Sky in my hearing will die hard!"

Since all Indians respected actions more than words, Little Horse gave still more force to his talk. He stood up and walked between his enemies and the campfire—a symbol that sent the rest of them back to their lodge, dragging the whimpering Medicine Flute with them. When a man crossed the fire like that, all fooling was past. The next word meant sure death for someone.

"Good work, brother," Tangle Hair said when they had left. "But we had best circle our robes with dried pods this night. And even if Touch the Sky really is still among the living, you don't need to be a shaman to know that he is up against the fight of his life."

"You took a nasty gash," Knobby said. "But by God, you come sassy! Boy, I swan, you'd wade into hell and come out with a land grant!"

"I sure as hell don't feel so damn sassy," Touch the Sky said, wincing as he touched the huge puff in front of his left ear. "I feel like death warmed over."

The two men had made a cold camp just past the site of the boulder strike. "Camp" was overstating the case—it was merely a protected nest among some boulders, more than half the space taken up by their horses.

"It was definitely Big Tree," Knobby confirmed. "I saw him jump down into that holler behind the ledge and get his horse. I shoulda busted a cap at him, but I was scramblin' to pull your raggedy ass out."

The last of the day's sunlight was bleeding from the sky. It was cold up here, and when the wind picked up it cut into their skin like knife blades.

"They're up there by now," Knobby said. "Waitin' on us."

Touch the Sky nodded glumly. Killing Big Tree down here would have saved them a lot of grief—not to mention, possibly their lives. But when had it ever been anything *but* hard against that red son of the Wendigo?

A sudden noise of rocks scraping sent both men into firing position. But it was only Knobby's claybank, shifting around.

"We goin' up tonight?" Knobby asked.

Touch the Sky shook his head. "No. You're right. We'll rest the whole night. I go up there now, I might as well hand them my weapons. Besides, Big Tree can see in the dark like a damn cat. I like dawn better. We set out an hour before sunrise, that should put us topside as the sun comes up. We'll need to get the lay of the place, figure out where we're going to stage out from. We can't make plans until we see what we've got to work with."

"Boy, either you're gettin' wiser, or my brain's gone soft and I can't tell shit from apple butter. Sounds like you're talkin' sense."

"I better be," Touch the Sky said as another spasm of pain washed over him. "Because luck and guts won't do it—not against Big Tree."

Before the glowing, blood-orange sun had dropped below the horizon, Big Tree and Poco Loco made a good mind map of San Sebastian.

The place was indeed made mostly of solid stone, huge blocks of fieldstone that must have been dragged into place by slave labor—probably Indian slaves. It was not really a town—just a small central plaza, its flagstones cracked and weed-infested now, surrounded by perhaps a dozen small stone dwellings.

"You were right," Big Tree confirmed, returning from a quick survey of the north face of the mountain. "Nothing but straight cliff. And so much scree at the base, even a mountain goat would need two days to climb it."

"What did I tell you?" Poco Loco boasted. "And you saw how the south face is. One narrow, twisting trail. It is the quarter of the full moon. If he comes up this night, our sentry will see him. Besides all that, he may be dead, for all you know. You said it looked like your trick killed him."

"Looked like," Big Tree repeated, "means nothing where that one is involved. When I hold his head over the bag, then I will believe he is dead. Who is watching the trail now?"

"Esteban himself. I wanted the best man there. Esteban is scared, but the rest are pissing themselves."

Big Tree nodded. "Esteban has a mouth on him, but I noticed he stays cold when the gunfire begins. Like you, Poco Loco. Both of you are too crazy to truly respect death."

The Mexican grinned, gold teeth gleaming in the setting sun. "Oh, I am no hero, amigo. There are women I wish to top, liquor to drink, men to kill—I am not eager to die yet. But this Cheyenne, he has challenged his tether too often and must reach the end of it. We are two of the best killers on God's green earth, Quohada! This is no Chapultepec Castle we have here, it is a natural fortress! The fight is ours to win."

Big Tree nodded. "You are right. But more will die."

He nodded down the little slope behind him. Besides Esteban, who was out of sight from here on guard duty, only three men remained alive: Lupe, Ernesto, and Juan. Each man now was on sentry duty atop one of the stone buildings.

"Should we leave the men out all night?" Poco Loco asked.

Big Tree shook his head. "Each by himself is a mere toy for Touch the Sky. At dark, we call in Esteban. Then all six of us fort up in the house we already fixed up. However, I suggest sending Esteban back out before dawn."

By "fixed up" Big Tree meant the solid rock walls they had built to block off the windows, whose wooden shutters had rotted long ago. They had been forced to kill two more dogs—wild, but not rabid this time—that had claimed the place.

Thinking of the dogs, Big Tree said, "There are too many droppings around here. We have not seen nearly all the dogs we are going to encounter."

Poco Loco raised the muzzle of his scattergun. "Why do you think my girl is out of her sling? But, amigo, it is an ill wind indeed that does not blow harm to someone—dogs are sunrise hunters. If our noble red man attacks at dawn as I feel he might, we will have one more ally on our side."

"Perhaps," Big Tree said. "But when it comes to killing that one, only a fool would bank on someone else doing the job. Sleep on your weapon. Better yet, do not sleep."

Chapter Thirteen

During the cold, fitful hours of rest, Touch the Sky could not always separate facts from dreaming.

Night had settled over the remote sierra called Blood of Christ like a change of climate. Rocks that, by day, had collected sun warmth now turned cold and miserable to the touch. Though bright moonlight kept them from total darkness, a powerful north wind shrieked down off the Colorado Plateau and continually blew rafts of clouds in front of the moon.

In his fitful sleep, Touch the Sky heard that wind howling. But he could not always tell it from the battle cries, from the cries of dying men and ponies, as dream images were placed over his eyes. Honey Eater appeared to him, and even in sleep he reached out to grasp the elusive image

that always disappeared like snowflakes melting
on a river.

And then there were the dogs.

Throughout the night Touch the Sky heard
them, not sure if they were part of the dreams or
part of the night: dogs howling, dogs barking,
dogs growling and snapping.

When he finally came awake, it was sudden and
all of a moment. Touch the Sky simply blinked
once, and the moment his eyes opened, he knew
where he was and what had to be done.

It had ever been so, for him. Other men might
drift through life and follow the forks in the trail
as they appeared; they could sleep late in the
mornings, bounce their children on their knees,
spend the warm mornings visiting with their clan
and soldier troops. For him, however, the cycle
was sure and relentless: The end of one battle
meant only the beginning of the next. Born in one
world, raised in another, now neither world accepted him.

Touch the Sky shook off his pensive mood even
as he sat up and began rolling his buffalo robe.
His experienced eye could tell, from the grain of
the light, that perhaps an hour remained before
sunrise.

"You awake, Knobby?" he said softly.

In fact the old man was sound asleep, for exhaustion had seeped into every pore of his aching,
worn body. But at the sound of Touch the Sky's
voice, Knobby sat up. Old reflexes made him
reach for his Kentucky rifle even before he came
fully awake.

"Course I'm awake," he groused. "Hell, I was only restin' my eyes."

Touch the Sky fed the remaining grain to the horses.

"We're going up without them," he decided. "It's not that far, and they'll just be sure targets. We can find cover better without them. That's not riding country up there, anyway."

"That's dyin' country up there," Knobby said. "Let's just hope it ain't us doin' the dyin'."

" 'Hope' your ass, old-timer. Let's make *sure* we don't do the dying."

Knobby grinned. "Well, cuss my coup! The pup is barkin' like a full-growed dog this morning."

Their moods slightly better now, both men quickly fell to on a final inspection of their weapons. Touch the Sky tied a short sling on his Sharps and strung it over one shoulder, his bow over the other.

They shared a few stale corn dodgers and a long drink of cool mountain water.

"Ready?" Touch the Sky asked.

Somewhere nearby a dog howled. Both men listened to the mournful sound as the ululating noise echoed from peak to peak in the morning darkness.

"Ready, goddammit," the mountain man replied. "Let's go make our beaver."

Esteban started violently when a hand touched his shoulder.

A shout of fear got stuck in his throat like a suppressed cough. He sat up, throwing his blankets aside, and groped for his big dragoon pistol.

"Easy, *'mano*," Poco Loco's voice calmed him. "I'm just telling you it is time for guard duty."

Esteban stared around the dimly lighted room. Big Tree was wide awake and probably had been all night. He sat, pistol in hand, watching the dwelling's only door. Lupe and Juan were fast asleep.

"*Jefe,*" Esteban protested. "Do we truly need a sentry out there? We are impregnable here."

"Here, yes. But tell me, brother. Do we never leave this place? We must go outside sooner or later, and it is crucial to know if that red devil has made it up here to this level."

"What if he came up during the night? What if he is already out there?"

Poco Loco, growing impatient, shook his head. "Big Tree knows him. He says no, he will come now. And you know how many dogs are holed up along the slope as you near the top. We would have heard a racket from them had he tried to slip by."

"Send Lupe," Esteban protested, trying to keep the whine out of his tone. "Chief, I have a bad feeling about going out there. Send Lupe or Juan."

"I *thought* you were a man," Poco Loco snapped. "That is why I want you out there."

Esteban, who could not stand a challenge to his manhood, forced himself to rise and wrestle on his boots, spurs jangling. He spun the cylinder of his gun, checking the loads.

"Position yourself just past the end of the trail," Poco Loco instructed him. "There is a jumble of rocks there that will provide good cover. You can't miss it if he comes up, amigo. A cockroach could not hide on that trail. It is pressed in on both sides by solid walls of stone. We will all take turns, two hours at a time."

"What if I see him?" Esteban asked.

"Most important is to fire a shot to warn us. I promise: From the time you fire a bullet until the time we appear will not be enough time to chew a biscuit."

For a moment, Esteban looked a little heartened. He was not a timid man, and the life of a pistolero had not left near-death scrapes remote from his experience.

But he recalled how Manuel's neck had been broken by the force of whatever struck his jaw, how Jorge's heart had come tumbling out of Poco Loco's fiber morral.

"I have a bad feeling about going out there," he repeated. But all he got for his protests were cold stares from Big Tree and Poco Loco—stares that said, take your chances out there like a man or we kill you for sure in here.

Esteban held his pistol at the ready as he lifted the heavy beam from the door and pushed it open, expecting death even as he did. But there was nothing outside, just a broad, gray, moonlit expanse of bare rock and stunted trees.

The wind rose to a howling shriek that sounded like all the devils in hell crying out at once. Esteban stepped out into the darkness, and Big Tree slammed the door shut behind him.

Touch the Sky had not realized, from farther down the slope, how constricted the only trail would grow as it neared its terminus in the cap-rock.

He had hoped to emerge on one of the flanks, sneaking around the sentry he was sure would be posted. But soon he realized that would prove impossible. The piles of scree and glacial moraine that crowded the narrow trail became solid walls of stone, so precipitous they were nearly vertical.

At most, Touch the Sky calculated with a sinking feeling of doom, the two men would have an area perhaps forty feet across from which they would be forced to debouch in the open. That wasn't very wide, and made things easy for a sentry in good position.

He and Knobby made good time while the last vestiges of night provided cover. They leapfrogged from boulder to boulder, one covering the other. Soon, they had angled around the last turn. Now the final, rock-strewn slope rose ahead of them.

Touch the Sky, pressing behind a jumble of rocks, spoke close to Knobby's ear.

"If you had to guard this trail, where would you dig in?"

Knobby nodded just to the left. "That cleft right there in that granite. Man could draw a bead on a pissant from there and hardly show himself."

Touch the Sky nodded, for his thoughts drifted the same way. The key to survival up here was to first clear that sentry post. From there the next priority would be shelter, some spot from which to operate while getting the lay of the place topside.

But rushing it was out of the question—ten men could not dislodge a coolheaded marksman from that opening, much less two. They could, of course, wait one entire day and try to ease past at night. But they were exposed here, vulnerable should anyone come down the trail.

Touch the Sky's warrior experience told him that only one strategy might work here: a distraction. Something the sentry wasn't expecting, something that would disrupt, just for a moment, his normal vigilance.

There still remained about forty yards of slope before they reached the vulnerable open stretch. As they set out to cover this final expanse, Touch the Sky again reminded old Knobby:

"Try like hell to avoid burning powder. One shot will bring Big Tree and the rest all over us like ugly on a buzzard."

The old man nodded. However, they had moved only a few feet before all hell suddenly broke loose.

With a savage snarl of rage, a yellow streak of fur leaped on Touch the Sky. His first thought, even as he reflexively tucked and rolled away from the leap, was that a mountain cat was about to kill him.

Claws raked his back, causing an explosion of fiery pain. Then he saw that his attacker was a dog as it missed him by inches and thumped into the rocks beside the trail.

Touch the Sky was at an awkward angle to defend himself, having been twisted off balance when he ducked from the dog. Desperately, as the fervid animal scrambled up with amazing dexterity and prepared to leap on him, fangs bared, the Cheyenne fumbled his knife from its beaded sheath and tried to set himself on the balls of his feet for balance.

The dog leaped, but Touch the Sky did not quite have time to get the knife up at the ready. A heartbeat later, Old Knobby flashed into view, giving a mighty swing to Old Patsy Plumb. The rifle's heavy stock slammed into the dog's skull even as it cleared the ground. The blow did not kill it, but as the stunned animal gathered itself, Touch the Sky drove his blade deep into its vitals.

Both men leaped for cover again, fearful that the racket had alerted the sentry above. But no one showed himself, and there were no warning shouts or shots.

"Good work, old-timer," Touch the Sky whispered. "You pulled my bacon out of the fire again."

Even as he spoke, Touch the Sky slid a flint-tipped arrow from his quiver. Knobby watched him notch it on his bowstring.

"The hell you doin'?" Knobby whispered hoarsely.

"I'm going to shoot a cloud," Touch the Sky answered.

Knobby, squinting as if the Cheyenne were a half-wit, glanced up into a sooty morning sky. The sun was still only a promise in the east, and any clouds were certainly invisible right now.

But it was true—the Cheyenne was aiming almost straight overhead. Knobby still hadn't caught his friend's drift, but a nervy little grin twitched the old man's lips.

"Good mornin' for cloud huntin'," Knobby agreed affably. "Make you a deal, sprout. You shoot one, and I'll skin the son of a bitch!"

* * *

Esteban had settled down since coming out to begin his stint on sentry duty.

Yes, he had indeed had bad forebodings about this day. But he felt safer here in the cleft than he did down below in the house. After all, it was an arduous climb just to reach this little pocket in the solid rock. Only one way up, and he could see every inch of it—as well as the end of the trail below.

He had heard a quick burst of snarls below, but Esteban hardly gave it a thought. The dogs were always fighting and snapping at each other. It hadn't been loud enough, or long enough, to signal intruders.

Esteban had finally settled down enough to build himself a cigarette with steady fingers. He had just put away his makings and was licking the paper when he heard it: a sudden clattering sound in the rocks.

Only—the noise came from *behind* him!

Panic held the Mexican immobile for perhaps ten heartbeats.

The last thing he had expected was noise from behind him. That must mean the intruders had already made it up here during the night.

He knew he had to look. Just a quick peek. If he poked his head out just for a moment . . .

No! No, he told himself. It was some kind of a trap. No one could be up there. Do *not* show yourself.

But again—another clattering noise. Definitely from behind this position.

He had to look. Taking a deep breath to steady

his resolve, Esteban nudged his head around the edge of the cleft and studied the terrain behind him.

Nothing. No one. Perhaps, after all, it was just—

He lost the thought when he saw it: An arrow lay broken among the rocks where it had landed.

A trick. He realized exactly what was happening, but just as he moved to duck back, a white-hot spike of pain replaced his throat. The arrow punched through his neck so hard it cracked into the rock face behind him. But Esteban was in no position to notice this as he hurled out of his safe nest and crashed into the rocks far below—the scream deep in his throat lost in a bubbling gurgle of frothy blood.

Chapter Fourteen

"*That* kissed the mistress!" Knobby gloated as he watched the Mexican come tumbling down out of the rocks, his neck skewered by Touch the Sky's arrow.

"Yeah, well, a kiss won't impress Big Tree. Let's recite our coups later," the Cheyenne said, breaking at a run for the end of the trail.

His rifle at a high port, Touch the Sky leaped over the dead sentry, stopping just long enough to grab the big dragoon pistol and stuff it in his sash. Then he raced for cover farther back in the caprock. Knobby followed him at a slower pace.

"You can just see San Sebastian from here," Touch the Sky said from behind the cover of a traprock shelf. He nodded toward the east. Perhaps two hundred yards away, the stone buildings could be glimpsed in a tight cluster.

"Look," Knobby said. "They got the other two Mexers up on the roofs. They ain't got a good angle on us here, but we won't get close by daylight. See how open it is around the buildings? Why, Katy Christ! You could have a Wild West show in that space."

Touch the Sky grunted affirmation, not liking the lay of things up here. Movement would not be impossible, but it would be risky. There were piles of rocks and some stunted scrub trees at this end. Closer to the little village, everything had been cleared off.

"I'd say trying to kill Big Tree in a built-up area is suicide," Touch the Sky decided.

"And I'd say that's about as wise as anything you ever spat out your feeding hole."

"And that Mexican boss with him—you saw his sawed-off. That's a man with experience at close-in killing."

"Uh-huh. So what do we do, tadpole? We ain't goin' to burn them out, that's for damn sure."

Touch the Sky was watching the body of the dead sentry. "No," he agreed. "So I think I'd better sneak back down there and hide that body a little better. His relief will be coming soon. I don't want him to be warned too early."

Knobby understood and approved with a nod. "When you can't bring Mahomet to the mountain, you bring the mountain to Mahomet. That'll be one more Mexer down."

If it works, Touch the Sky thought. If it works. But how often could the pitcher keep going to the well before it finally went dry? Besides, even with one more Mexican down, Big Tree was still alive.

Killing these Mexican bandits was still only hacking at the branches of the tree of evil. Killing a man like Big Tree, however, was like digging up the roots.

Touch the Sky put all thoughts away from his mind. Then, making sure he stayed out of sight of those guards, he slipped down to hide the dead man.

"I don't like it," Poco Loco said quietly to Big Tree.

Under cover of daylight and the sentries, the two old comrades had come outside to reconnoiter. Now they stood at the edge of the plaza, staring toward Esteban's sentry post.

"I told him to use his mirror," Poco Loco said. "I told him to flash the all clear every hour to Juan and Lupe. But there has been nothing since the sun came up."

"Nothing? You are sure of this?"

Poco Loco frowned at this challenge to his capabilities. "Am I sure? Does a big-titted woman sleep on her back? Of course I am sure. I have watched every minute."

"Could he be asleep?" Big Tree asked.

Poco Loco shook his head. "Not Esteban. He is a good man. Besides, he was too scared to sleep."

Big Tree definitely did not like what he was hearing. His eyes squinting, deep in speculation, he scanned the rugged terrain to their west. If a man paid him to describe his idea of what the moon must be like, Big Tree would describe that godforsaken waste of scree and twisted growth.

"You think he is up here?" Poco Loco said,

dread clear in his voice. "You think he killed Esteban?"

That was precisely what Big Tree thought. But he could see that even Poco Loco, tough as jerked leather, was on the verge of panic. And in fact, Big Tree himself was beginning to taste the bitter bile of fear.

"We will know soon enough," the Comanche said evasively. "It is time to send Esteban's relief."

Poco Loco's obsidian eyes goaded Big Tree. "Care to go yourself, war leader?"

Big Tree refused to rise to the bait. He merely replied calmly, "You go, *jefe*."

"I never miss breakfast," the Mexican replied tersely before turning and cupping his hands around his mouth.

Poco Loco shouted up toward the nearest roof. "Lupe! Time to relieve Esteban!"

Lupe, a feckless-looking man with a drooping teamster's mustache, shook his head. "Send Juan," he said.

"Fuck your mother!" Juan shouted from a nearby roof. "Esteban has not shown his hide since sunup! I am not going out there!"

Big Tree's .44 fairly flew into his fist. He snapped off a round, and Lupe's sombrero fluttered to the ground. The scared Mexican scrambled down.

"All right!" he shouted. "I am going. But I have a wife and children in Saltillo. Juan should go!"

Juan *will* go, Big Tree thought. All in good time. Juan, Lupe, and the rest were merely bones being thrown to the wolf. Bait to make that wolf show himself, just once . . .

*   *   *

Lupe did not feel so frightened so long as he was in clear sight of San Sebastian. But as the deserted settlement dropped from view, his pulse began to thud in his ears.

Death stalked this place, palpable as wet fog to the skin. Lupe's grandfather swore that, just before a man's appointment with the Grim Reaper, he would see an image of himself, his second self, as it said good-bye. And Lupe had indeed seen himself in a dream last night, standing beside his bedroll and gazing at himself with the saddest expression.

Slowly he picked his way through the scattered rocks, his carbine clutched tight against his right hip in case he had to snap-shoot.

A sudden skittering sound sent him to his knees, weapon pointed toward the noise. But it was only a windblown leaf tumbling over the rocks.

Santísima Maria, he said softly, crossing himself as he again cautiously rose to his feet and resumed his journey toward the pinnacle with the cleft in it, a natural sentry post. It did not seem likely, he thought, that a man as sharp as Esteban could be killed in such a secure post.

Perhaps, after all, Esteban was just asleep?

Lupe kept his gaze in constant motion, scanning the terrain around him, as he moved closer and closer to that cleft pinnacle.

"Esteban?" he called out. "Esteban, are you up there?"

"Where the hell else would I be?" answered a grumpy voice in Spanish.

Relief surged through Lupe. He was so glad to

hear his comrade answer that he hardly noticed how different Esteban sounded—but perhaps a long stint out here in the raw night wind would work on any man's throat.

"You fool," Lupe upbraided him even as he scrambled up the rock toward the cleft. "You were supposed to send mirror flashes back. Did you fall aslee—?"

His voice trailed off when Lupe got his first glimpse into the cleft. Then, all in one confused moment, several things happened simultaneously.

It had been old Knobby whose voice he heard answering in Spanish. And it was to have been Touch the Sky's job to kill the new arrival—a routine and silent kill with an arrow the moment he showed himself.

But just as Touch the Sky released his bowstring, Lupe's careless left foot came down on a loose stone, not solid rock ledge. The Mexican tumbled back roughly but harmlessly to the flat below even as Touch the Sky's arrow sliced past his face.

Touch the Sky cursed, groping for his knife and hoping to get one clear toss at the sentry before he could gain his feet again.

But Lupe instinctively squeezed off a warning round, and Touch the Sky realized it was too late now—Big Tree and the other two were warned.

Cursing again in English, Touch the Sky pressured the dragoon pistol's trigger and the big gun bucked in his hand, a round punching into Lupe's vitals. One more down, Touch the Sky told himself, but now the element of surprise was lost.

"I'll get his weapon," Touch the Sky told Knobby. "You climb down the other side and start looking for a good place for us to hole up. The odds are down to three to two now, so I doubt they'll try to flush us."

"Big Tree ain't no hero," Knobby said. "You think he might just run?"

Touch the Sky nodded. "That's exactly what I think. So wherever we hole up, let's make sure we're in sight of the trail. That's the only way down from here. And I'll tell you right now, Big Tree won't leave this mountain alive unless I'm dead."

"Unless *we're* dead," Knobby corrected him. "I'm tired of that red bastard's ugly face. That sumbitch needs killin', and he needs it bad."

Touch the Sky knew they could see the pinnacle from San Sebastian with field glasses. Since his presence up here was no longer a secret, he didn't bother to sneak as he climbed down to Lupe's body and confiscated his weapon and bandolier.

Indeed, he even stared toward the houses and grinned his mocking, defiant grin as he knelt with one knee on Lupe's neck to hold the head in place. He made a quick outline cut around the scalp, then snapped it loose with one powerful tug and held it aloft.

"That stinking, flea-bitten, gut-eating savage!" Poco Loco fumed, handing the glasses to Big Tree. But the Comanche only waved them off—his sharp eyes had seen the mocking demonstration out in the rocks.

"*Jefe!*" Juan called out from the roof. "What do

we do now? That red devil is up here!"

"I have a remarkable grasp for the obvious, numbskull," Poco Loco shouted up to his man. "Stop blubbering like a woman and be a man!"

But in a quieter tone, the Mexican gang leader said with malevolent fury to Big Tree, "I should kill you, Quohada. When you rode in among us, I had ten men. Now look up there on the roof! That is the scrag end of my gang! And we are trapped here between the sap and the bark with a killing machine!"

"You could try to kill me," Big Tree agreed calmly. "And perhaps you could do it. You are no man to take lightly, Poco Loco. But there is also a very good chance that I would kill you first, true?"

Poco Loco said nothing. Some truths were too obvious for comment.

"But only think," Big Tree continued. "With me dead, you lose your best chance for survival against the Cheyenne."

"Why?" Poco Loco retorted. "It is you he is after."

"Are you so sure, amigo? If that is so, then why am I still alive while all of your men except one is carrion?"

Poco Loco met this with a gloomy silence.

"We two stand our best chance," Big Tree continued, "if we stand back to back against Touch the Sky. As for your men. You yourself admitted such as they are easily replaced. Keep your courage in your parfleche, Poco Loco, and we will soon be three thousand dollars richer."

Poco Loco considered all of this for some time before he finally nodded. "But what can we do?"

he protested. "We are low on food, supplies. We can't stay up here forever, hiding."

"No," Big Tree agreed, nodding. His weathered face was inscrutable as he turned and slowly stared up toward Juan.

"What we need," Big Tree said, "is to lay a trap with our remaining piece of bait."

Poco Loco was still distracted by his own worries and did not see where the other man was looking. "What bait?" he snapped peevishly.

"The bait up on the roof pissing himself in fright like a squaw woman."

Poco Loco met his eyes. "You mean—deliberately sacrifice Juan?"

Big Tree's lips twitched in the beginning of a grin. "You sound horrified. The tall one has killed your men anyway. Why should we not exact a profit from his killing? Besides—consider the alternative."

After some time, Poco Loco nodded. "As you say, Quohada. It is him or us."

Big Tree noticed the slight emphasis on the word "us," but kept a straight face. He knew Poco Loco as well as he knew himself. So he knew full well the Mexican would look out for his own hide and no one else's—exactly as Big Tree meant to do.

Both men fell silent, and in the distance rose the lone, mournful howl of a dog.

Chapter Fifteen

"Anyhow," Knobby said, gnawing on the last of his jerked meat, "they wa'n stupid enough to send another guard out."

A long day was almost behind them, and now Sister Sun sent their shadows slanting sharply toward the east. They had taken shelter behind a hastily erected breastwork of stone, almost certain that attempting to hide was a waste of time—the remaining trio were not likely to attack. Indeed, Touch the Sky thought—that would be preferable to the infinitely more dangerous job of routing them out.

Both men had taken turns snatching what sleep they could, for they were certain this night would bring trouble. Big Tree knew full well that a trapped man's chances for survival went down dramatically the longer he waited. Nor was the

Comanche one to let his enemy determine the battle plan.

"No, they sure as hell don't want to lose another gun," Touch the Sky said. "And that's the only reason they aren't sending a guard out. Big Tree and his Mexican friend with the scar are both two seeds from the same pod. They'd pick a baby up in a second if it would stop a bullet from hitting them."

Touch the Sky paused, listening to it: another long, drawn-out howl from the pack of wild dogs that obviously lived around here. Sometimes he could hear them snarling and fighting among themselves; other times he saw their eyes glowing furtively in the dark, watching him and Knobby.

"Them sons a bitchen dogs might go for the horses," Knobby said. "If we leave 'em alone too long."

Touch the Sky knew the old-timer was right. But this whole mission was a fool's venture, and the horses were just one more reckless chance that had to be taken. Besides, he was worn out from fretting all the things that might go wrong.

All day long, and during his fitful naps, Touch the Sky had been haunted by the pretty face of Honey Eater. Did the mother of his child still live, in spite of that smoke signal? Hope was a waking dream, and Touch the Sky clung to hope like a drowning man in a raging river, clinging to driftwood.

The wind, cooling rapidly now as the sun went down, suddenly rose with a howling shriek, slicing through their inadequate clothing.

"Colder 'n a landlord's heart," Knobby muttered.

Touch the Sky knew the old trapper was suffering bad, though Knobby said nothing. Touch the Sky was only one third his age, yet his bones were weary. What must it be like for Knobby? Despite his guilt at Knobby's suffering, however, Touch the Sky was glad the old man had insisted on coming along. That wild dog might well have gotten its fangs into his throat if Knobby hadn't knocked it ass over apple cart. It felt good to have a veteran frontiersman riding shotgun.

And besides—weariness didn't matter. This mission had to be completed. In one sense, it didn't matter if Honey Eater was dead or alive. Big Tree had to die. Touch the Sky knew that, knew it down deep in his bones the way a Baptist knew Jesus.

Again Touch the Sky examined the darkling sky, calculating how much time remained before the Red Raider of the Plains made his next move.

"Won't be long," Knobby assured him. "What's come so far has just been pee doodles. Before this night is over, boy, me 'n' you are gonna stir up a Fandango!"

"Juan," Poco Loco said casually, "go feed the horses before it gets too dark."

Juan, nursing the last of his mescal in the corner, looked up sullenly. Now that so many of his comrades were dead, he blamed Poco Loco and that savage Big Tree. But this was no time to mutiny—the two he hated were also his only hope for survival.

"Can't it wait until morning?" Juan said.

"No," Poco Loco added, "because we might be making our break tonight, and we'll need rested mounts."

This news seemed to hearten Juan. He set his bottle aside, grabbed his rifle, and moved to the front door. He waited until the other two were covering him, then threw the door open.

Nothing outside except the gray-black, barren twilight. Wind howled, making Juan grab to save his Sonora hat. But the prospect of leaving this hellhole heartened him. He went on outside and aimed for the corner of the plaza where the horses were tethered.

It had been Big Tree's idea to lure one of the wild dogs with meat, then tie it up as a sentry near the horses. Any attempt to approach them set the dog yapping like it was right now.

"I didn't think we'd ever get rid of him," Poco Loco said the moment the door shut behind the departing man. Poco Loco was glad now that they could talk. "What is the plan?"

"It won't be fancy," Big Tree assured him. "There isn't enough time to get creative. I think the best plan is to make the Cheyenne think we're making a break down the trail under cover of darkness. We'll wait until Juan comes back, then we'll act like we're planning it all out with him."

Big Tree interrupted himself for a moment when he heard it: a snarling clamor of dogs. Either fighting among themselves, or angry at the human intruders up here. Hearing the noise made him nervously recall the odd prophecy of a Kiowa medicine man: *Keep the dog far hence that is foe to Big Tree!*

"We will pretend," Big Tree continued, "that our best chance is to escape down the trail one at a time."

Big Tree tapped the deck of cards Poco Loco always carried in his vest pocket. "We will draw cards to see what order we ride out in. And, of course, you will stack the deck so that Juan rides first."

Poco Loco grinned, revealing yellow teeth like two rows of crooked gravestones. *"Claro.* The Cheyenne will strike at Juan, and when he reveals himself, we will strike at the Cheyenne."

Big Tree nodded. "As I said, nothing fancy. But at least it is a plan."

Poco Loco nudged the door open. He could see Juan hurrying back across the plaza, head bent into the wind.

"It is," he agreed. "This has been a hard bargain for me so far, Quohada. I have traded nine men for a chance at that Cheyenne, and still I have not had my opportunity. Let us hope number ten will be the charm."

It had better be, Poco Loco thought. Because if the Cheyenne kills number ten, he will turn to numbers eleven and twelve. And one of those numbers is mine.

Shortly after sunset, Knobby shook Touch the Sky from a light doze.

"Heigh-up, sprout! They're movin' out on us!"

Touch the Sky sat up quickly and glanced around the protective wall of the stone breastwork. It was true: There was enough moonlight to see that the trio in the house were cinching up.

"Only one way they can be going," the Cheyenne said quietly. "And that's down the mountain."

" 'Lessen it's a trap," Knobby remarked.

"Of course it's a trap," Touch the Sky said. "I know Big Tree like I know the Bighorn country. It's a trap. They were hoping we'd attack by now. They didn't provision themselves for a siege. So now they're drawing us out for a clear shot at us."

"Should we hang back and drop their horses?" Knobby suggested.

Touch the Sky shook his head. "Bad idea. What if ours are dead or gone when we get below?"

Knobby grunted affirmation. Something else occurred to him. It wasn't just dogs that posed a threat to their horses.

Knobby said, "They *will* be dead if them bastards ride down—they'll make sure they're dead. And us trapped on foot in the middle of goddamn nowhere."

"Check your powder," Touch the Sky told his partner. "We'll play it like this. We need to see what they've got planned before we move. But we don't dare let even one of them very far down that trail, or we can kiss our horses good-bye. You'll go back to that cleft in the pinnacle and watch them from there. I'm going down the trail a ways before they get started."

Knobby frowned. All his warrior instincts warned him against the folly of dividing their force, small as it was. But Touch the Sky's next words made good sense and showed he was thinking like his enemy.

"My hunch goes like this. They'll send the last member of the gang down the trail, hoping to draw me out for a shot. If that doesn't happen soon after their man hits the trail, they'll figure it's safe, and they'll hit it too. That's where you come in, Knobby. You can't get a plumb bead in this light. But you can shoot close enough to scare Big Tree back off that trail. I don't care about either of the Mexicans. It's Big Tree I want."

The old trapper nodded, clicking back the Kentucky rifle's mule-ear hammers. "Then it's Big Tree we'll get. Let's get 'er done, boy."

Juan didn't really mind it when he drew the low card and had to ride first down that trail. That way, at least, his back trail would be covered. Of course, the prospect of hitting that trail left him with a sickening loss-of-gravity tickle in his stomach. But he would rather harrow hell than sit up there in that stone coffin, waiting for death to strike.

"Give your mount his head and let him set the pace," Poco Loco informed him. "I will ride down behind you, about five minutes after you set out. Keep a good eye to the shadows—that is where he will lurk."

Poco Loco and Big Tree had taken up positions among the boulders heaped at the head of the mountain trail. Each man took advantage of what moonlight there was, scouring the surrounding terrain.

Juan made sure he had a primer cap on the nib of his rifle. "See you down below," he called out bravely, swinging up into the saddle and nudging his mount toward the trail.

Touch the Sky heard the Mexican descending long before he came into view.

As the exhausted Cheyenne crouched there in the darkness beside the narrow trail, his optimism began to grow. For it had occurred to him: If he killed the next man silently and efficiently enough, he might simply be able to wait right here for Big Tree, too, to come down.

He left his knife in its sheath. A knife was excellent in a grappling struggle or for ground fighting—and most fights quickly ended up on the ground. But a stabbed man often cried out. In Touch the Sky's experience, clubbing a man to death was the most silent way to kill.

His Sharps was solid, with a good length. He took off his leather shirt and wrapped it around the barrel, using it to get a good grip.

The steady clip-clop of approaching hooves grew gradually louder. The Cheyenne touched his medicine pouch as he sent a silent prayer to Maiyun, God of the red man, asking him once again to make him worthy to be a warrior.

Big Tree waited, in the first minutes after Juan rode down, for the crack of a rifle, the shriek as an arrow pierced Juan's lights, the frenzied nickering of a panicked horse. But down below all was silent—ominously silent, like the dead calm before a gully washer.

Maybe, just maybe, it's clear, Big Tree thought. A hard little nubbin of hope began to grow inside him. The Cheyenne could be asleep or holed up.

Think that way, a sudden inner voice warned him, *and you'd best sing your death song.*

Big Tree glanced through the darkness toward Poco Loco's rock. Best to stick to the plan, the Comanche thought. Let Poco Loco go next. He didn't want that crazy bastard behind him anyway—not now, with the Mexican nursing a grudge against him.

Besides, if Touch the Sky was down that trail, as Big Tree believed, then it was best to have two men go first—that was two chances Touch the Sky would be killed before Big Tree got to him.

Sometimes the balance of opportunity could shift in an eyeblink. Touch the Sky had been in enough battles to realize that. Seldom did raw power or pure attrition bring on a victory—almost always, one side or the other got a sudden break.

These thoughts, however, were very remote from his mind as the Cheyenne raised his rifle like a club in the darkness, preparing to strike at the descending enemy.

At that moment, a heavy bank of cirrus clouds blew away from the moon. Unnoticed by Touch the Sky, a tiny piece of silver trim on his rifle stock glinted for a moment in the moonlight.

Juan, descending with his head swiveling from side to side, felt his heart skip a beat when he saw something flash beside the trail—up ahead, just to the right. Had there been enough time, he might have ruined the opportunity by halting his horse and thus warning the bushwhacker.

Instead, with the reflexive quickness of a cat, he

nudged his rifle off his saddle tree and let the barrel swing right and down. At the same moment a shadowy figure loomed up, Juan pressured his trigger, and an orange spear-tip of muzzle flash illuminated—point blank—the war face of the Cheyenne!

Chapter Sixteen

That shot, Poco Loco told himself the moment he heard a rifle speak its piece down the trail, that was Juan's old British trade rifle. He recognized its distinctive, high-pitched crack.

He waited for more shots, but none came. There was only a long, suspenseful pause, then the recognizable clatter of iron-shod hooves on rock as Juan's pony made its escape down the trail.

Quickly, knowing his life depended on the right decision, Poco Loco tried to read these clues.

If the Cheyenne had struck first, silently as usual, then it was unlikely Juan would have gotten off a shot. On the other hand, if Juan got lucky first, it would make sense that his rifle was the only one Poco Loco heard.

Hope sounded its notes in his breast as Poco Loco continued to mine this vein of thought. After all, Juan could indeed have gotten lucky. Though a bit of a coward, he was intelligent and careful; more important, that red killer had to be getting careless by now. This ruthless pace, the exhausting ride, the lack of sleep or good shelter—even the best men courted death once they got careless on *la frontera*.

But if Juan had killed the Cheyenne, why would he escape down the trail instead of coming back up here to gloat and brag with his comrades? It didn't make—

Christ Jesus!

All of an instant, Poco Loco understood: It was the Cheyenne's head! That was why Juan was running like a bat out of hell. Every one of the men knew the head was worth three thousand in gold to some gringo named Hiram Steele.

That pause after the shot: Juan must have taken just enough time to decapitate the corpse.

Originally, Poco Loco had meant to wait until Big Tree went down first, knowing that was his best protection against the Cheyenne killing machine. Now, however, it was suddenly more important than life itself to get down that trail first and lay hands on that treacherous son of a bitch Juan.

Big Tree struck a lode when he said it: A man in Mexico toiled for thirty cents a day. To hell with any gang—Poco Loco could take that head himself and live in comfort down in Guadalajara.

Poco Loco slid his scattergun from its sling on his side and broke open the breech to make sure both bores were loaded. Then, his face urgent with the need to hurry, he raced for his mount.

Desert Manhunt

Big Tree, who knew Touch the Sky far better than did his Mexican companion, interpreted events quite differently.

The Comanche, too, hunkered behind his boulder, had been surprised to hear Juan's British rifle crack first. It was not Touch the Sky's way to allow his prey a shot.

However, the pause after the shot, then the clopping of escaping hooves, answered the mystery for him.

Big Tree's ear was trained for survival. He recognized immediately, from the sound, that the escaping horse was riderless. A riderless horse sent up a different pattern, less rhythmic.

And if Juan's horse was riderless, the best conclusion was that Touch the Sky had killed the rider.

Big Tree saw Poco Loco break for the trail, and a cynical grin tugged at his lips. Let the Mexican run to the trap. Big Tree had other ideas.

There was a chance Poco Loco would succeed where Juan had not. He was a steady man in a crisis, never getting so agitated that he forgot to make every shot count—one bullet, one enemy.

If a shotgun roared, Big Tree thought, that might be a hopeful sign. But he didn't count on it. Instead, he meant to take a leaf out of the Cheyenne's own book. He was going to take cover behind the very rock breastwork that Touch the Sky had used. Big Tree had one chance, and he knew it. That was to make the Cheyenne come to him, not the other way around.

If Poco Loco did kill the Cheyenne, all well and

good. Big Tree would be out nothing except an unnecessary vigil.

Big Tree glanced around uneasily, wondering about the second man with Touch the Sky. He hadn't seen any sign of him up here, but that didn't mean he wasn't there.

For a moment the big renegade flinched when a sudden howl sounded, very nearby this time. Those damned dogs were obviously moving in.

Moving quickly from boulder to boulder, Big Tree raced west toward the breastwork.

Shit-oh-dear, Knobby thought as he watched all the action below. What the hell's going on?

He could not see well enough from his position in the cleft pinnacle to draw a bead on anybody. If he could have, he'd have been happy to back-shoot Big Tree. But when that gun went off down the trail, the old man had watched the Mexican *jefe* take off for below. Soon after that, Big Tree broke for the rocks to the left of the trail.

Tarnal hell, Knobby thought. Talk about being trapped between a rock and a hard place! He had to make a decision. Stay right here and wait for Matthew, thus keeping an eye on Big Tree, or break for below and see if Matthew was still alive but perhaps injured.

If Matthew came up soon enough, that would be best, Knobby thought. Then he could simply warn the Cheyenne, as he broke up from the trail, that Big Tree was waiting in their old hiding place.

But although Knobby forced himself to wait patiently, Matthew didn't show.

"Katy Christ," he muttered out loud. Much as

he hated to make the wrong move, he had to check on the sprout. If he was lying down there bleeding to death . . .

His tired old bones flaring in protest, Knobby clutched Patsy Plumb close to his chest and began climbing down from his post.

Touch the Sky had no idea that the Mexican named Juan had seen him. Only the reflexive instincts of a honed warrior made him tuck and roll just as that rifle went off.

The Cheyenne had no time for grace or to plan his leap. Even as a bullet creased his skull, thumping it like a mule kick, he simply threw himself down and forward—right into the forelegs of Juan's pinto.

Already the Mexican was squaring around for a second shot, and Touch the Sky knew it. Desperate, he relied on an offensive move perfected by beleaguered Cheyenne warriors in the days before they rode horses but their enemies did.

A horse was very vulnerable in its thin forelegs. Touch the Sky wrapped himself around these as he fell, twisting hard left to topple the horse, then immediately hard right to avoid its falling weight.

He succeeded in making the horse crash down hard, snapping Juan's spine as it did. But the tired brave could not quite roll completely clear himself. The horse's big head cracked down hard on Touch the Sky's, and though he fought against it, the darkness of oblivion washed over him even as the horse struggled to its feet and escaped down the trail.

*   *   *

Poco Loco had not bothered with discretion, coming down the trail after that thieving bastard Juan. All the Mexican gang leader could think about was laying hands on that valuable Cheyenne head.

But he reined in abruptly, heart leaping into his throat, when he saw the tangled mass of limbs in the trail just below him.

Startled, he slid to the ground and moved his horse between himself and the two men who lay sprawled ahead. Thus protected, Poco Loco stared at the inert forms while he cautiously waited and assembled all the details.

What he saw made his scarred visage divide itself in an ear-to-ear smile.

Juan was dead as a Paiute grave—that was clear from the impossible angle of his spine. The Cheyenne, however, was merely unconscious. Poco Loco could see the steady, strong rising of his muscle-corded chest.

"Juan, old chum," Poco Loco said softly, chuckling, "I owe you an apology. Good work, hombre! Your death has handed me three thousand *yanqui* dollars in gold."

Poco Loco quickly hobbled his horse foreleg to rear. Then he walked closer, lining the muzzle of his scattergun up with the unconscious Cheyenne's heart. It was essential not to mar the face. Poco Loco wanted this Hiram Steele to see exactly whom he was paying for.

Poco Loco took up the trigger slack, squeezed harder, and then came a booming roar. A heartbeat later, the back of Poco Loco's skull lifted off like the lid of a cookie jar, and the Mexican folded to the ground dead.

"Kiss for ya, you ugly beaner bastard," Knobby said out loud from his position about twenty yards farther up the trail. Patsy's top muzzle still gave off curls of smoke.

Then, his fingers crossed, Knobby moved forward to see if Matthew still belonged to the world of the living.

Matthew did indeed belong to the living. But he had also cracked his head hard under the impact of the falling horse. When Knobby asked the groggy Cheyenne what tribe he belonged to, he answered with a straight face, "Coyotero Apache."

Any other time, Knobby might have laughed out loud. But it wasn't particularly funny right now—not with Big Tree prowling the area and Touch the Sky too stove up to be moved.

Knobby did what he had been doing all his life—made the best of a bad situation.

Moving very carefully and slowly, he dragged his friend as far off the trail as he could. Then the old man, grunting and cursing, kneecaps popping, gathered up rocks and built another breastwork for defense. At least, Knobby consoled himself, they knew Big Tree had only one direction from which to approach them.

That done, Knobby managed to shoot a mountain goat. He butchered out the hindquarters, the only part that made good eating. He built a fire under some rocks and cooked the meat on it.

By daylight Touch the Sky had come to, though his head throbbed in painful explosions every time he tried to move. Knobby, who had guarded the trail during the long hours, took a turn at sleeping. Off and on they relieved each other, sleeping and fortifying their strength with fresh meat.

Knobby had already informed Touch the Sky that Big Tree was holed up behind their old breastwork. Touch the Sky considered it for some time. Finally, he saw how things stood.

"Big Tree would have come down by now," he told Knobby, "if he wanted to force my hand against him. But he's not. He's deliberately holding back. He's giving me the choice."

The old man nodded. "I figgered it by now, too. He's putting it to you as straight as it could be put. You can ride out now and live out your days. Or you can go up topside and maybe dig your own grave. Been almost a whole day now he's been waiting. It's time to post the pony or pull stakes."

Touch the Sky nodded. Neither one of them doubted what Touch the Sky intended to do.

"I'm going up there at sundown," Touch the Sky said. "This has dragged out too long, and I'm sick of it. But there's no good reason for you to wait here. If you do, he could kill you if—well, if he whips me. And there's a good chance he can. I hate that bastard, but I'm the first to say he fights like five men."

"Ahh, t' hell with you," Knobby said with exaggerated nonchalance. "I ain't goin' nowheres. Get your blanket ass up that slope and kill that red son, wouldja, boy? Pretty quick I got to get—your ma and pa would like to brand the year-old colts *some* goddamn time. Used to was, you didn't take so damn long to kill a worthless varmit!"

Touch the Sky rallied at this show of bravado,

for it was exactly the kind of show that his own band would have put on at a time like this. When death breathed down a man's neck, that was the time to joke and make light of it with companions. Otherwise terror might defeat him even before the battle.

But bravado was to make a man feel courage. It would not kill Big Tree. Touch the Sky settled into his robe, watching the light in the sky, waiting.

Although Knobby had recruited their ponies safely, Touch the Sky chose to go up that slope silently on foot.

The sun had settled behind the horizon, leaving the mountains shrouded in their customary cloaks of cold darkness. But a three-quarter moon and a star-spattered sky provided ample, if ghostly, light.

Touch the Sky's double-soled moccasins were silent on the sharp-edged rocks. He ascended the trail like a shadow, gliding silently, making progress without appearing to be moving.

Sweat broke out on his back, causing the sharp gusts of wind to slice into him. He could feel the reassuring weight of his Sharps in his hands, the knife tucked into his sash. Though he was aware that Big Tree was any man's equal, Touch the Sky did not feel great fear—only a calm, fierce determination to rid the world once and for all of this Comanche menace.

Staying behind rocks, he eased up off the trail onto the flat above. He glanced left and immediately spotted them in the moonlight: dead dogs.

Several of them, scattered around in front of the breastwork. Two more living dogs, evidently scavenging carrion, skulked off as the Cheyenne appeared.

Looks like Big Tree had himself a night of it, Touch the Sky thought absently. But was he still behind that breastwork? Or had he moved east and reoccupied the town itself?

Cautiously, moving from boulder to boulder, Touch the Sky began to ease across the barren expanse. He was just moving past the lookout pinnacle, the one with the cleft in it, when Touch the Sky heard it: a low, simmering growl that originated from overhead.

Dog close by, he thought, glancing overhead. But when he did, a shock slammed into him like a body blow.

Big Tree stood crouched in the cleft, ready to spring on him! But the shock of seeing the Comanche in his present condition completely stunned Touch the Sky and blunted his instincts to react.

Big Tree had torn all of his clothes off, and his naked body was savaged by tooth marks. Obviously he had been attacked by a pack of wild dogs. Just as obviously, judging from the white foam pouring down his chin, at least one of the dogs that bit him was rabid.

It was not a man who hurled himself down onto Touch the Sky, but a wild and savage animal. The Cheyenne was slow to move, and the big Comanche's weight threw him hard to the ground.

Touch the Sky's rifle was useless, close in like this. He threw it aside, even as he fought to avoid

Big Tree's gnashing teeth, and wrestled his knife from its sheath.

Big Tree didn't need a weapon. Rabid as he now was, his teeth had become all the weapons he needed. Touch the Sky knew that he was worm fodder if he let his enemy bite him.

Like all insane men, Big Tree's prodigious strength was nearly doubled. He easily trapped the Cheyenne under him, though Touch the Sky had managed to get a hand under his chin so he could keep Big Tree's mouth rammed shut.

Thus they struggled, Big Tree wearing him down, Touch the Sky unable to get his knife hand around for a killing blow. Slowly, inexorably, the Cheyenne's left arm weakened. With an abrupt snarl of triumphant rage, Big Tree threw his head back and bared his dripping fangs for the final plunge.

Touch the Sky's last image was of his beautiful wife, drained pale as moonstone from loss of blood. And then Arrow Keeper's voice came back to him from the hinterland of memory: *Tell me how you die, and I'll tell you what you're worth.*

And all of a moment, Touch the Sky knew that he could not let his adversary triumph—could not let this miserable, literal dog's death be the final statement on his own worth as a man.

With a howl of rage that drowned out Big Tree, the Cheyenne arched his back hard and threw the Comanche aside. In a heartbeat his knife hand was free, Touch the Sky leaped, and then heat flooded his hand when he shoved the obsidian blade deep into the renegade's warm and beating heart.

*   *   *

Many sleeps later, as twilight glittered to life over the Powder River Cheyenne camp, a lone rider on a coyote dun appeared on the final ridge overlooking the camp.

"Hii-ya!" he shouted to the rest, announcing his arrival with the war cry. "Hii-*ya!*"

Touch the Sky, who had no way of knowing that false word of his death had been sent north, could not understand the look of overwhelming joy on the faces of his men as they raced up the slope to greet him.

He knew only, with no shame in his heart, that he was crying hot, copious tears when he saw her: Honey Eater, walking, then running, out of their tipi to greet him. Little Bear ran out behind her, shouting for his father.

Honey Eater still walked among the living. In that moment Touch the Sky forgot everything else except his gratitude to the Holy Ones who had kept her alive. He raised his lance toward the heavens, and he found himself saying the same words his friend Little Horse had said at the beginning of this epic journey: *There is hope.*

CHEYENNE

JUDD COLE

Don't miss the adventures of Touch the Sky, as he searches for a world he can call his own.

Cheyenne #14: Death Camp. When his tribe is threatened by an outbreak of deadly disease, Touch the Sky must race against time and murderous foes. But soon, he realizes he must either forsake his heritage and trust white man's medicine—or prove his loyalty even as he watches his people die.
_3800-5 $3.99 US/$4.99 CAN

Cheyenne #15: Renegade Nation. When Touch the Sky's enemies join forces against all his people—both Indian and white—they test his warrior and shaman skills to the limit. If the fearless brave isn't strong enough, he will be powerless to stop the utter annihilation of the two worlds he loves.
_3891-9 $3.99 US/$4.99 CAN

Dorchester Publishing Co., Inc.
65 Commerce Road
Stamford, CT 06902

Please add $1.75 for shipping and handling for the first book and $.50 for each book thereafter. NY, NYC, PA and CT residents, please add appropriate sales tax. No cash, stamps, or C.O.D.s. All orders shipped within 6 weeks via postal service book rate. Canadian orders require $2.00 extra postage and must be paid in U.S. dollars through a U.S. banking facility.

Name_____
Address_____
City _____ State_____Zip_____
I have enclosed $_____in payment for the checked book(s).
Payment <u>must</u> accompany all orders.☐ Please send a free catalog.

CHEYENNE

JUDD COLE

Follow the adventures of Touch the Sky as he searches for a world he can call his own!

#3: Renegade Justice. When his adopted white parents fall victim to a gang of ruthless outlaws, Touch the Sky swears to save them—even if it means losing the trust he has risked his life to win from the Cheyenne.

__3385-2 $3.50 US/$4.50 CAN

#4: Vision Quest. While seeking a mystical sign from the Great Spirit, Touch the Sky is relentlessly pursued by his enemies. But the young brave will battle any peril that stands between him and the vision of his destiny.

__3411-5 $3.50 US/$4.50 CAN

CHEYENNE
JUDD COLE

Born Indian, raised white, he swore he'd die a free man.

#10: Buffalo Hiders. When white hunters appear with powerful Hawken rifles to slaughter the mighty buffalo, Touch the Sky swears to protect the animals. Trouble is, Cheyenne lands are about to be invaded by two hundred mountain men and Indian killers bent on wiping out the remaining buffalo. Touch the Sky thinks it will be a fair fight, until he discovers the hiders have an ally—the U.S. Cavalry.
_3623-1 $3.99 US/$4.99 CAN

#11: Spirit Path. Trained as a shaman, Touch the Sky uses strong magic time and again to save the tribe. Still, the warrior is feared and distrusted as a spy for the white men who raised him. Then a rival accuses Touch the Sky of bad medicine, and if he can't prove the claim false, he'll come to a brutal end—and the Cheyenne will face utter destruction.
_3656-8 $3.99 US/$4.99 CAN

#12: Mankiller. A mighty warrior, Touch the Sky can outlast any enemy. Yet a brave named Mankiller proves a challenge like none other. The fierce Cherokee is determined to count coup on Touch the Sky—then send him to the spirit world with a tomahawk through his heart.
_3698-3 $3.99 US/$4.99 CAN

Dorchester Publishing Co., Inc.
65 Commerce Road
Stamford, CT 06902

Please add $1.75 for shipping and handling for the first book and $.50 for each book thereafter. NY, NYC, PA and CT residents, please add appropriate sales tax. No cash, stamps, or C.O.D.s. All orders shipped within 6 weeks via postal service book rate. Canadian orders require $2.00 extra postage and must be paid in U.S. dollars through a U.S. banking facility.

Name_____
Address _____
City _____ State _____ Zip _____
I have enclosed $_____ in payment for the checked book(s).
Payment <u>must</u> accompany all orders.□ Please send a free catalog.

DON'T MISS THESE CLASSIC *LEISURE* WESTERNS!

Pepper Tree Rider by Jack Curtis. After the Civil War, Elizabeth Hamilton does the best she can to hold the Lazy H together, for with her husband gone, she has only her nine-year-old son, an elderly vaquero, and a sickly brother to help her. But she's fighting a losing battle against time and rustlers, and soon there'll be nothing left. But she hasn't counted on another rider coming to the Lazy H–one who is ready to risk everything he has to protect her.

___4270-3 $3.99 US/$4.99 CAN

The Whipsaw Trail by Ray Hogan. No matter how hard John Buckner tries, he can't get the railroad to pay him. So when he robs the railroad's payroll from the bank, he figures he is only taking back what is rightfully his. Railroad detective Henry Guzman doesn't see it that way, and sets out with a posse to get his man. Now, with the law on his track, Buckner's trail is leading him straight into renegade Indian territory.

___4258-4 $3.99 US/$4.99 CAN

WHITE APACHE

DOUBLE EDITION
The West is Taggart's land–his gun his only friend!
JAKE McMASTERS

Bloodbath. They are a ragtag bunch of misfits when Taggart finds them, a defeated band of Apaches–but he turns them into the fiercest fighters in the Southwest. And then, on a bloody raid into Mexico, some of his men rebel, and Taggart has to battle for his life while trying to reform his warriors into a wolf pack capable of slaughtering anyone who crosses their path.

And in the same action-packed volume...

Blood Treachery. From the Arizona Territory to the mountains of Mexico, Taggart and his wild Apaches ride roughshod over the land. Settlers, soldiers, and Indians alike have tried to kill White Apache, but it'll take cold cunning and ruthless deception. And when a rival chieftain sets out to betray Taggart's fierce band, they learn that the face of a friend can hide the heart of an enemy.

___4271-1 $4.99 US/$5.99 CAN

Dorchester Publishing Co., Inc.
65 Commerce Road
Stamford, CT 06902

America's Favorite Western Storyteller!

Free Range Lanning. Andy Lanning is a decent man–although he can ride and shoot with the best of his leather-tough family, he will just as soon walk away from trouble. Then his Uncle Jasper pushes him into a fight with a town hothead who ends up lying in the street while Steve rides out of town with a posse on his trail. And before the posse can string him up, Andy will get tough–the toughest they will ever see.

___4268-1 $4.50 US/$5.50 CAN

Wooden Guns. Big Jim Conover was the toughest hombre and the fastest gun in the Western mountains. But his reputation as a ruthless gunfighter drove him away from home. Now, five years later, he returns, a broken and crippled man. But the injury has transformed Jim into an honorable man. Trouble is, to everyone in town Big Jim is still the leather-hard gunman he used to be...and they have some old scores to settle.

___4228-2 $4.50 US/$5.50 CAN

Dorchester Publishing Co., Inc.
65 Commerce Road
Stamford, CT 06902

Please add $1.75 for shipping and handling for the first book and $.50 for each book thereafter. NY, NYC, PA and CT residents, please add appropriate sales tax. No cash, stamps, or C.O.D.s. All orders shipped within 6 weeks via postal service book rate. Canadian orders require $2.00 extra postage and must be paid in U.S. dollars through a U.S. banking facility.

Name_____
Address_____
City_____ State _____ Zip_____
I have enclosed $_____ in payment for the checked book(s).
Payment <u>must</u> accompany all orders. ❏ Please send a free catalog.

CHIRICAHUA

"Some of the best writing the American West can claim!"
—Brian Garfield, Bestselling Author of
Death Wish

Led by the dreaded Geronimo and Chatto, a band of Chiricahua Apache warriors sweep up out of Mexico in a red deathwind. Their vow–to destroy every white life in their bloody path across the Arizona Territory. But between the swirling forces of white and red hatred, history sends a lone Indian rider named Pa-nayo-tishn, The Coyote Saw Him, crying peace–and the fate of the Chiricahuas and all free Apaches is altered forever.

The Spur Award–winning Novel of the West

___4266-5 $4.50 US/$5.50